## SIX-GUN SHOWDOWN

A Winchester erupted into life behind Madam Henrietta's parlor house, blasting away in a roll of gunpowder thunder.

Landrum jerked his .44 from its holster and bounded through the front door and into the parlor, Glidinghawk at his heels. Several of the house's girls screamed.

Two of Madam Henrietta's men appeared at the top of the stairs, guns in hand. Landrum went down on one knee as a slug shrieked close by his ear. He triggered the Colt and saw one of the men go spinning away with a shattered shoulder. Beside him, Glidinghawk fired and dropped the other one.

Well, they'd never intended the plan to be real subtle, Landrum thought.

Simply put, Powell's Army was here to bust hell out of the place and pick up the pieces later.

# POWELL'S ARMY
# BY TERENCE DUNCAN

### #1: UNCHAINED LIGHTNING (1994, $2.50)
Thundering out of the past, a trio of deadly enforcers dispenses its own brand of frontier justice throughout the untamed American West! Two men and one woman, they are the U.S. Army's most lethal secret weapon—they are POWELL'S ARMY!

### #2: APACHE RAIDERS (2073, $2.50)
The disappearance of seventeen Apache maidens brings tribal unrest to the violent breaking point. To prevent an explosion of bloodshed, Powell's Army races through a nightmare world south of the border—and into the deadly clutches of a vicious band of Mexican flesh merchants!

### #3: MUSTANG WARRIORS (2171, $2.50)
Someone is selling cavalry guns and horses to the Comanche—and that spells trouble for the bluecoats' campaign against Chief Quanah Parker's bloodthirsty Kwahadi warriors. But Powell's Army are no strangers to trouble. When the showdown comes, they'll be ready—and someone is going to die!

### #4: ROBBERS ROOST (2285, $2.50)
After hijacking an army payroll wagon and killing the troopers riding guard, Three-Fingered Jack and his gang high-tail it into Virginia City to spend their ill-gotten gains. But Powell's Army plans to apprehend the murderous hardcases before the local vigilantes do—to make sure that Jack and his slimy band stretch hemp the legal way!

*Available wherever paperbacks are sold, or order direct from the Publisher. Send cover price plus 50¢ per copy for mailing and handling to Zebra Books, Dept. 2383, 475 Park Avenue South, New York, N.Y. 10016. Residents of New York, New Jersey and Pennsylvania must include sales tax. DO NOT SEND CASH.*

# POWELL'S ARMY
#5 ROCKY MOUNTAIN SHOWDOWN
## TERENCE DUNCAN

**ZEBRA BOOKS**
**KENSINGTON PUBLISHING CORP.**

ZEBRA BOOKS

are published by

Kensington Publishing Corp.
475 Park Avenue South
New York, NY 10016

Copyright © 1988 by Terence Duncan

All rights reserved. No part of this book may be reproduced in any form or by any means without the prior written consent of the Publisher, excepting brief quotes used in reviews.

First printing: June, 1988

Printed in the United States of America

# CHAPTER ONE

Celia Louise Burnett had seen mountains before, but still the sight of the Rockies in the distance thrilled her—so much, in fact, that she had a hard time concentrating on the cards in her hand.

"I'm in," the man opposite her said, pushing money into the center of the table. He glanced up, met the pretty young redhead's gaze, and smiled.

Celia looked quickly down at her cards and tried to will herself not to blush. She swayed slightly in her chair as the train rounded a bend. The Rockies were still visible through the windows of the railroad car. Celia told herself sternly to ignore all the distractions—natural and otherwise—and concentrate on the game.

If only Major Devlin Henry hadn't been so damned handsome!

To Major Henry's left, a tall, grim-visaged Omaha Indian stared at his cards and grunted as he decided to stay in the hand. It was a bit unusual to find an Indian playing poker with white men, but Gerald Glidinghawk's money and manners were just as good as anyone's. And so far Glidinghawk had lost consistently, which made the other players that much more tolerant of his red skin.

Celia knew that Glidinghawk was being careful not to reveal that he knew her. As far as the other four players around the table were concerned, the redheaded young woman and the dour Indian were total strangers.

That was the way they wanted to keep it.

Glidinghawk was probably unhappy with her, Celia thought. She knew damn well that Landrum would be. She was sure to hear about it later, once the train reached Denver.

The game continued at a steady, pleasant pace as the train rolled southwestward. The club car where the game was taking place was almost like a saloon on wheels, and Celia felt right at home. There was a small bar on one wall, behind which a white-jacketed bartender dispensed drinks. Several booths lined the other wall and gave a semblance of privacy for the couples who huddled within them. The other tables were full for the most part, and there was a comfortable buzz of conversation and laughter in the air, along with the smoke from fine cigars.

Celia knew she should have stayed in her seat in the car just ahead, should have traveled in decorum like the well-bred young lady she was supposed to be. But when Major Henry had mentioned the poker game in the club car, Celia had been unable to resist. There was something deep within her that resonated to the lure of games of chance and skill.

"Let's just up it a bit, shall we?" she said now, pushing a sizable bet into the center of the table. "I believe that's fifty to you, Mr. McDermott."

Cyrus McDermott sighed heavily. During the brief self-introductions the players had carried out before starting the game, he had revealed that he owned a successful hardware store in Denver and was on his way back from a buying trip in Kansas City. He was a born merchant, full of caution and avarice.

McDermott glanced at his cards again and grimaced, but he said, "I'll stay."

Celia let her eyes roam around the table, taking in the other players. Besides Glidinghawk, McDermott, and Major Henry—she already wanted to refer to him as Devlin—there were two other men in the game. Curt Selmon was a rancher, relatively successful from the look of him. The final player, Oliver Blaine, was obviously a gambler. His fancy dress and his deft touch with the cards revealed his profession. No doubt he made this journey often and joined in all the games along the way.

The bet was back around to Devlin Henry, who raised it yet again. Glidinghawk's mouth twitched disgustedly, and he threw in his cards. "Injun no damn fool," he said in self-mockery, which drew a chuckle from several of the other players.

Devlin didn't laugh. He seemed to take the game quite seriously. But there was still a slight twinkle in his eyes when he glanced at Celia.

She had known him only a few hours, but already it seemed as if they had been friends for years.

He had introduced himself to her that morning in the dining car, being quite the gentleman about it. He had noticed that she was traveling alone, he had said, and he offered to accompany her to whatever hotel she was stopping at when the train arrived in Denver. There was not a hint of anything improper about the offer, Celia sensed. She had a feeling that he would have made the same suggestion had she been a white-haired, sixty-year-old lady.

Of course, considering his broad shoulders and crisp dark hair and dashing mustache, Celia might not have minded at least a hint of something improper. . . .

They had sat together during the morning, dined together at midday, then both had gravitated back here to the club car for this friendly poker game. Celia had been aware a time or two of the veiled warning looks sent in her direction by Landrum Davis, but the tall Texan was not supposed to know her, any more than Gerald Glidinghawk was, so there wasn't much Landrum could do about the matter except send the Omaha along to keep an eye on her.

Besides, as long as she did her job, Landrum had no right to complain about her choice of companions. And it might help to get to know Major Henry better.

He was, after all, heading to Denver to join the very commission that was bringing Powell's Army to Colorado Territory.

The dispatch from Lt. Colonel Amos Powell assigning them to this case had reached them in Montana Territory. Celia, Landrum, and Glidinghawk, along with the fourth member of their team, Preston Fox, had just brought a dangerous mission to a successful conclusion—successful for the most part, anyway.

Faced with the threat of being disbanded had the mission gone badly, Powell's team of undercover civilian investigators was back in the good graces of the adjutant general's office, at least for the moment. All of them knew quite well that things could change rapidly should they have trouble with this new assignment, however.

Which was one more reason Celia should have resisted the temptation to join this game, she mused. But as she laid down a full house and raked in a good-sized pot, an undeniable thrill shot through her. She might be the daughter of a well-respected army officer, but she was a gambler at heart.

The only thing that would improve the current situation was if she could go over to that bar and get a drink. Something stronger than the too-sweet brandy which she had allowed herself a little earlier.

The sun was dipping down toward the jagged crests of the mountains to the west. The train would not pull in to the Denver & Pacific station in the territorial capital until after dark. That was the main reason Devlin Henry had offered to escort her.

Denver was a fairly young town, growing steadily, full of all kinds of people—including some who were not too nice, even to visiting young ladies.

Especially visiting young ladies as attractive as Celia.

As the deal passed to Celia, she heard Cyrus McDermott scrape his chair back. "This game is just too steep for my blood," the businessman muttered. He turned and headed for the bar.

He hadn't been gone thirty seconds when a new figure stood beside the table, a hand on the empty chair. "Mind if I sit in?" the newcomer asked.

Celia looked up to see a young man dressed like a cowboy. The range clothes were clean but well worn. The man's Stetson was pushed back from a lean, dark face with sharp eyes. There was something unsettling about the grin on his face and the set of his jaw.

Devlin Henry was regarding the stranger with equal scrutiny. After a moment, he nodded. "All right with me," he said. The rancher, Selmon, grunted assent, as did Glidinghawk.

The gambler, Oliver Blaine, smiled up at the cowboy. "Please have a seat," Blaine said smoothly. "That is, if the young lady has no objection."

"How about it, ma'am?" The cowboy smiled cockily down at Celia.

Her instincts told her that this young man might represent trouble, but she couldn't explain that to the others. If they saw no reason not to welcome the cowboy into the game, she couldn't very well deny him the empty chair.

"Please join us," Celia said, forcing a tiny smile onto her face.

"Name's Ben Malone," the cowboy said as he sank into the seat. He pulled a roll of bills from his pocket and dropped it onto the table in front of him. "Don't know what your limit is in this game, but I reckon I can afford it."

No one was going to ask him where he had gotten the money. That would have been rude to the point of being a shooting insult. But the other players didn't have to wonder for long. Ben Malone turned out to be a talkative young man.

"Just took a herd into Dodge City," he told them. "Brought them beeves all the way up from San Antone. I didn't feel much like heading back to Texas right now, though, so I decided I'd come see me some mountains." He nodded toward the train's windows and the Rockies beyond. "They're mighty impressive."

"That they are," Devlin agreed.

Celia was dealing the cards. The pasteboards left her hand with practiced ease. She was more at home dealing faro, had in fact done just that during Powell's Army's first mission together. But she had quite a bit of experience at poker, too.

Celia took the first hand she dealt, then Devlin Henry won the next two. As she won the next hand, she saw Ben Malone looking narrowly at her out of the corner of his eye. So far he hadn't come close to winning, although he had plunged heavily on a couple of hands and seemed to think he had them. At the rate he was going, the roll of bills wouldn't last him too long.

His luck seemed to turn as the deal passed on to him. He won a hand, then Glidinghawk and Selmon each took one before Malone won two more. The young cowboy had just about recouped his losses.

When it was Devlin's turn to deal, Malone's newfound luck seemed to desert him once again. Celia won most of the hands for a while, and when she wasn't raking in a pot, Devlin was.

Malone kept looking from Celia to Devlin and then back again. His face became darker, his eyes narrow with suspicion as he squinted at his cards. He flung the hand down in disgust.

"Seems like the only way I can get a good hand is if I deal it myself," he snapped.

Oliver Blaine chuckled humorlessly. "Comments like that might tend to make people a bit suspicious of you, my friend."

"Take it easy, Malone," Selmon put in. "This is a friendly game."

"Hell, I'm as friendly as the next fella," Malone shot back. "Reckon I should have said the only way I can get an honest hand is to deal it myself."

Slowly and carefully, Devlin Henry put the deck of cards down on the table. There was still a smile on his face, but his features were tight with controlled anger now.

"There's no call for that kind of talk," he said. "And no place around this table for either rash accusations or profanity. Not with a lady present."

Malone glanced at Celia. "Sorry, ma'am," he said, sarcasm dripping from his voice. "Reckon I was out of line to hint that you and this prettyboy major are in cahoots and cheating."

"You certainly were," Celia said icily. She glanced at Glidinghawk and read the concern in his eyes. It was bad enough that she had gotten involved in this game in the first place. It would be even worse if some sort of trouble came out of it.

Malone nodded. "I should have come right out and said it," he sneered. He looked back at Devlin. "You and this *lady* are cheating, mister.

What are you going to do about it?"

Devlin wasn't smiling now. He stood up, his face dark with anger. "Why, you young—" he began, his hands curling into fists.

Malone was suddenly springing up and back, knocking his chair over behind him, his hand flashing toward the big gun holstered on his hip.

Celia screamed.

# CHAPTER TWO

Malone was fast, no doubt about it. His gun was clear of its holster, the barrel tipping up toward Devlin, when Celia moved with a speed born of desperation.

The cowboy was only a couple of feet away from her. She reached out, acting instinctively, and planted her hands on his hip. She shoved as hard as she could.

The push was just enough to throw him off balance. The gun in his hand blasted, the racket of the shot deafening in these close quarters, but the bullet came nowhere near its intended target, Major Devlin Henry. Instead the slug thudded harmlessly into the wall of the car.

The other occupants of the club car went diving for cover. There were more screams from the ladies present.

Malone caught himself before he could fall and

tried to bring the gun back into line. But Celia's action had given Devlin the chance to lunge around the table into striking distance. The major's fist lashed out, and hard knuckles crashed into Malone's jaw with a sickening smack.

The cowboy's head was snapped around by the blow. He stiffened, and the pistol slipped from suddenly limp fingers. Malone pitched forward, bouncing off the table and then sprawling bonelessly on the floor of the car.

Devlin rubbed his knuckles and grimaced. His hand was already starting to swell. He shook his head and grinned at Celia. "Thanks," he said. "That lunatic would have drilled me if you hadn't shoved him."

Celia swallowed and then licked dry lips. Her ears were ringing from the gunshot, and her nerves were stretched taut by the sudden violence. "He . . . he was crazy, all right," she said, her voice hoarse.

"Of course he was," Oliver Blaine said. "I assure you, I would have known about it if you or the major had been, shall we say, tilting the odds too much in your favor. Despite what our young friend on the floor might have thought, this is an honest game."

Curt Selmon stood up wearily and glanced at Glidinghawk. "Come on, mister," the rancher said to the Omaha. "Let's drag him out of here."

The train's conductor appeared, either having heard the gunshot or been summoned by the club car's bartender. He was a burly man with a face like a middle-aged bulldog, and he asked, "What's the trouble here?"

"No trouble now," Devlin told him. He nodded to Malone's body as Glidinghawk and Selmon stooped to grasp the unconscious cowboy. "That man thought he was being cheated at cards. He drew his gun and fired a shot. With the help of this young lady, I subdued him."

The conductor glanced dubiously at Celia, as if unsure what help she could have been in taming a wild young cowboy. Then the trainman looked at Blaine and said, "Don't I know you?"

"Indeed you do, sir. Oliver Blaine, at your service. I ride these rails quite often."

The conductor grunted. "And this fella thought you was cheating him?"

"No," Devlin said quickly. "He accused the young lady and me of working in concert."

Blaine raised one eyebrow mockingly. "You see, conductor, I'm not the only one who has aspersions cast upon his honesty."

The conductor nodded heavily. "All right, go back to your game if you want to." He gestured to Selmon and Glidinghawk. "Bring that boy back to the caboose. I'll have a brakeman keep an eye on him and see that he don't get into any more trouble."

Malone was hauled out, and Devlin sat down opposite Celia again. She hoped some color was coming back into her face by now. She must have

17

looked a sight immediately after the ugly incident.

"Well," Blaine said, squaring up the small stack of bills in front of him, "perhaps it would be best if we resumed our game some other time. My luck was not running too well this evening anyway."

"That's fine with me," Devlin replied. "I'm not sure Miss Burnett is in the mood for any more cards, and I know I'm not. Getting shot at doesn't help a man's concentration."

"Indeed not," the gambler chuckled. He stood up and touched the brim of his hat. "Good evening, Miss Burnett."

Celia nodded. "Good evening, Mr. Blaine."

Blaine headed for the bar, leaving Celia and Devlin sitting alone at the table. The major leaned forward, a concerned look on his face as he regarded her. "Are you sure you're all right?" he asked.

Celia smiled. "I'm fine now. I certainly never expected such a thing to happen, though."

"You probably saved my life."

Celia felt herself blushing again. "Really, I didn't . . . didn't even have time to think."

"Then your instincts certainly came in handy for both of us." Devlin shook his head. "These hotheaded frontiersmen! Malone's like most of the cowboys I've seen. They shoot first and think later, if at all."

Celia lowered her voice as she said, "Major

Henry, there is one thing you can do for me, if you don't mind."

"Of course not. But I think it's time you called me Devlin."

She smiled weakly. "All right . . . Devlin. I . . . I could certainly use a drink."

He started to stand up. "Some more brandy?"

Celia shook her head. "No. A *drink*."

A grin tugged at the corners of Devlin's mouth. "Of course. You just wait right here."

He went to the bar and came back a moment later with two glasses of whiskey. Things were returning to normal in the car now, and Celia knew as she reached for the whiskey that she shouldn't be drinking it out in the open like this. It didn't really fit in with her cover identity. But then neither did poker playing.

She swallowed the liquor quickly, ignoring any looks the other passengers might have been giving her. It burned pleasantly going down, then kindled warming embers in her belly. She already felt better as she set the empty glass on the table.

"Shall I escort you back to your seat now?" Devlin asked.

Celia nodded. "That would be fine, I think."

They stood up and linked arms. Celia kept her eyes downcast as Devlin led her back to the car where her seat was located. As they went out through the rear door of the club car, a cold wind pushed against them in the open space between cars. In this late fall of 1875, winter was not far off. Here at the foot of the Rockies, there would be plenty of snow and ice and frigid blasts before the warming breezes of spring arrived again.

Now, however, the weather was still not too bad in Colorado Territory. Although Celia shivered slightly at the chill in the air, her lightweight coat was sufficient for the moment. With any luck, perhaps Powell's Army would be finished with its mission and able to move on to warmer climes before winter really settled in.

As Celia settled into her seat, Devlin dropped onto the bench opposite her. She returned his smile, then glanced past him. Several seats ahead of her, Landrum Davis had turned enough to cast an unhappy stare in her direction. The Texan turned away quickly, not wanting to appear too obviously displeased with her.

Devlin pulled a watch from the pocket of his blue uniform and opened it. "We ought to be getting into Denver in another half hour or so," he said. "Where did you say you'd be staying?"

"The Royal Hotel," Celia replied.

Devlin shook his head. "I'm not familiar with it. The commission I've been assigned to is quartered at the Colorado House, but I've never been there either. In fact, I haven't been to Denver before. Heard plenty about it, though."

So had Celia. Amos Powell had warned her to be careful while she was there. Denver might be the territorial capital now, but not too many years before it had been little more than a mining camp, full of men with all the bark still on, as Amos had put it. He suspected that below the surface it hadn't changed too much.

Celia said none of that to Major Henry. "I'm sure it's a fine city," she began, then broke off as the door of the car opened behind her, then shut quickly. Glidinghawk strode past her and joined Landrum, sitting down opposite the Texan and beginning to speak in a low voice.

Landrum glanced over his shoulder again, glaring in Celia's direction, and she knew that the Omaha was telling Landrum about the commotion in the club car.

She was sure Landrum would have plenty to say about it when they reached Denver.

Celia made small talk with Devlin Henry for the next few minutes, still enjoying his company but unable now to put the forthcoming mission out of her mind. She kept a sweet smile on her face and hoped he wouldn't notice how distracted she had become.

He was telling her about his childhood back in Ohio when the conductor came through the car, sonorously intoning, "Denver! Next stop, Denver! Denver in five minutes!"

By leaning closer to the window, Celia could peer forward and see the lights of the town beginning to appear up ahead. Full night had fallen now; the mountains in the distance had disappeared in shadow.

"Why don't you give me the tickets for your

baggage?" Devlin asked. "I'll go claim them for you."

Celia retrieved the tickets from her bag and passed them over to Devlin. "Thank you," she said. "I've only got the two, one trunk and a smaller bag."

"I'll attend to them, don't worry. I'm sure there are probably carriages for hire around the station. I'll engage one to take us to the Royal Hotel."

Atop the train, brakemen slowed the cars as the train rolled into the Denver & Pacific station. The car in which Celia was riding gave a slight lurch as it came to a stop. There was a sound of metal clashing as the entire train shuddered to a halt.

Devlin stood up and took Celia's arm once again. She avoided the gazes of Landrum and Glidinghawk as she and the major disembarked from the train. Once they were on the platform, Devlin said, "You go into the station out of the wind. I'll get our bags and be right with you."

She nodded. "All right, Devlin."

As he moved off toward the baggage car, Celia joined the other passengers going into the station. She saw Glidinghawk heading toward the baggage car as well. Suddenly, Landrum was beside her, hissing an angry whisper at her.

"Stay in your room when you get to the hotel," he ordered her, then he let the flow of the crowd carry him away before she had a chance to answer.

Celia's lips tightened. The lean Confederate was

the nominal leader of Powell's Army, based simply on age and experience, but she thought he sometimes took things too seriously. However, all the members of the team were still alive after four dangerous missions. That said something for Landrum's leadership abilities—and good luck.

Abruptly, she spotted another familiar face inside the station. Preston Kirkwood Fox, the fourth member of the group, had been traveling in another car, one in which the seats were a bit less expensive. He wore a cheap suit and a bowler hat, and he looked like what he really was—an Easterner still a little out of place in the West.

He also looked angry. The young second lieutenant had started out as the liaison officer between Powell's Army and the adjutant general's office. He had become a full member of the team following a debacle of sorts in Dodge City in which his cover identity had been compromised. Following that, he had played a major part in the just-concluded mission in Montana.

Now, in what Celia was sure Fox regarded as a demotion, he was having to keep a low profile. Landrum, Celia, and Glidinghawk all had cover identities established for this Denver assignment. Fox's orders were for him to hold himself in reserve to be used however the rest of the team deemed necessary.

Knowing Preston Fox, Celia was certain that he hated it.

He looked none too happy as he made his way

through the station, but except for an instant's glance, he paid no attention to Celia. Fox was improving at this game, Celia thought. When he had first started working as their liaison, he had been almost as much of a danger to them as the villains they were seeking to uncover.

Devlin appeared carrying Celia's bag and his own valise. A porter was behind him with Celia's trunk. He stuck Celia's bag under the arm that was carrying the valise and used his now-free hand to take her elbow.

"Come along," he said heartily. "I've got a carriage waiting outside."

The porter loaded the baggage into a boot at the rear of the carriage while Celia and Devlin settled into the seat behind the driver. Devlin leaned forward and said, "Do you know where the Royal Hotel is?"

"Sure thing, Major," the driver replied. "That where you want to go?"

"Yes, it is." Devlin moved back next to Celia. The carriage seat was not overly wide, and the two of them were forced to sit rather close together.

Celia didn't mind that at all.

For one thing, it was warmer this way. For another, she liked Devlin Henry. He struck her as a decent man, and there was no denying his attractiveness. Being this close to him made her feel slightly light-headed. Of course, that could have been from the whiskey she had drunk earlier.

But she didn't think so.

Devlin pointed out the dome of the territorial capitol as they passed within a few blocks of the impressive structure. The city was busy and well lighted, even at this hour of the evening. Most of the stores they passed were still open. Celia wouldn't have been surprised to see the saloons doing a good business, but it appeared that the entire town was booming.

The Royal Hotel, while not the most elegant hostelry in Denver, turned out to be a solid-looking building of stone and wood. When the carriage drew up in front of the place, Devlin helped Celia down and then had to unload the bags himself when no porter or doorman appeared.

"Wait here for me," he told the driver, slipping the man a bill. "I'll be going on to the Colorado House."

"You bet, mister," the driver replied.

Inside the lobby of the hotel, the air was a bit stuffy. Celia went to the desk with Devlin at her side. Behind the desk was a narrow-faced man in shirtsleeves and vest. He coughed and then nodded to them.

"What can I do for you folks?" he asked.

"I believe you have a room for the lady," Devlin spoke up before Celia could reply. "It should be in the name of Miss Celia Burnett."

"Oh, yes, Miss Burnett." The clerk nodded, shuffling through some cards on the desk and coming up with the proper one. He indicated the register and said, "If you'll just sign in, Miss Burnett."

As Celia did so, the pen scratching annoyingly, the clerk smiled at Devlin and continued, "And you, Major, will you be staying with us also?"

"I'm afraid not," Devlin told him. He didn't volunteer any more information about the commission he was joining at the Colorado House. "I assume your establishment is a nice, quiet place for a young lady of good breeding to stay?"

"Of course, Major."

Celia was glancing around the lobby. Evidently the hotel didn't have a bar. She tried to hide her disappointment.

"I'll have a boy get your baggage, Miss Burnett," the clerk said. He took a key from the pegboard behind him and extended it. "That'll be Room 12, at the top of the stairs." He held the key about halfway between Celia and Devlin, unsure which one of them was going to take it. There was the faintest hint of a smirk on his face.

Devlin put an end to that by taking the key and then handing it to Celia. He touched the brim of his hat and said, "I hope I shall be seeing you again, Miss Burnett. It was a pleasure traveling with you."

Celia smiled at him. "A pleasure indeed, Major. Thank you for your assistance."

He nodded, pressed her hand, then strode briskly to the door of the hotel. As he opened it and went out, another man came in. Landrum Davis spotted Celia standing at the desk and started in that direction.

Celia turned quickly to the clerk. "You'll have that boy bring up my things?" she asked.

"Yes, ma'am," the man assured her. "He'll be up in just a few minutes."

"Thank you." Clutching the key, Celia went to the stairs and started up them toward the second floor. Landrum couldn't very well come chasing after her, not in front of the clerk.

The showdown would come soon enough, Celia thought. No point in hurrying it along.

and went on, not realizing how far behind
Over at the Kells shanties the old man had
started in that direction.

Otto turned quickly to the door. "Don't think
that boy is paying any attention," he said.

"Yes, he is," said the man-starved boy. "He'll be
up in just a few minutes."

"Too bad," said Grimthin, the boy could win to
the shack and settled up there forever. The several
boats, standing doubtful, very still came closing
swifter, too, through them all his ears...
of. The powerboat would come, on board then,
thin it... but none an onnight a shape—

# CHAPTER THREE

Celia had been in her room about a half hour when the soft knock came on the door. She had unpacked most of her things, hanging the clothes in the big wooden wardrobe on one wall. The rest of the furnishings were sparse—a rather tarnished brass four-poster, a dresser with a cracked mirror, and a ladder-backed wooden chair. At least there was a rug on the floor.

As the knock was repeated, Celia closed her eyes and blew a stray lock of red hair off her forehead. She knew who was out there in the hall, and she knew what was about to happen.

Postponing the meeting wouldn't do any good. She had begun to think about going out for some dinner, but that would have to wait.

Celia opened the door, and Landrum Davis slipped through into the room. Gerald Glidinghawk was right behind him. As Celia shut the door, she asked, "Where's Fox?"

"He'll be here in a few minutes," Landrum replied. "He's staying at a boardinghouse in the next block. But until he gets here and we can go over the orders from Powell—"

"I know," Celia cut in. "You've got a few things to say to me."

"Damn right!" Landrum exploded. "I swear, Celia, is it that hard to keep from drawing attention to yourself?"

She crossed her arms and tried to maintain control of her emotions. "You're a fine one to talk, Landrum Davis," she said coolly. "We're not even supposed to know each other, and yet here you are in my room, shouting at me."

"I am not shouting—" Landrum began in a loud voice.

"There is no one in either of the rooms next to this one," Glidinghawk put in quietly. "I checked before Landrum and I entered here. There is only a slight chance that anyone will overhear us."

Landrum nodded. "That's right. Now, what did you think you were doing on that train? You're supposed to be a proper, respectable young lady, and yet there you were playing poker and getting mixed up in a shooting scrape."

"The shooting was not my idea," Celia said, heat entering her voice. Landrum was starting to blame her for things over which she had no control. "Besides, I thought it would be a good idea to get to know Major Henry, since he is going to be part of the commission we've been sent here to investigate."

Landrum snorted. "Get to know him, eh? Is

that what you call it?"

Celia flushed at the implication in his tone. It was the same one that had shown in the smirk of the man behind the desk downstairs. She knew that Landrum was fond of her, maybe a little too fond at times, but he had no right to be jealous.

"Major Henry was always a perfect gentleman," she said stiffly.

"You sound disappointed," Landrum snapped.

Glidinghawk chuckled grimly. "If you two don't quit sniping at each other, you'll do the enemies' job for them."

Before he could say any more, another knock sounded on the door. Celia glared at Landrum for a second, then went to the door and opened it just enough to see out. Preston Fox's angry face looked in at her.

Celia stepped back and opened the door to admit him. "Come on in, Preston," she said bitterly. "You might as well take your turn abusing me."

Fox appeared puzzled as he insinuated his lean form into the room. "Why would I want to do that?"

"I don't know," Celia told him. "But Landrum seems to be enjoying it quite a bit."

Landrum took a deep breath as Celia closed the door behind Fox. "Listen," he said sincerely. "Lord knows I understand the lure of a drink and a good poker game, Celia. I've sat in on a lot more of them than you have. But now that we seem to have things working fairly well for the team, we don't want to ruin them by being careless."

Celia started to reply hotly, then subsided instead. She had been careless, and she knew it. But Landrum didn't have to take such a damned superior tone! Anyway, there was a good chance that her relationship with Devlin Henry might turn out to be valuable before this job was over.

"All right," she said, more to put the matter behind them than to constitute an admission of guilt, "I'll be more careful in the future. Why don't we talk about how we're going to proceed now that we're here?"

Landrum nodded. "Good idea." He reached inside his jacket and brought out a thick leather pouch filled with maps. Inside it was a concealed pocket, and he took a sheet of paper from the little hiding place. He smoothed it out, then handed it to Celia.

"You'd better look over Amos's dispatch again," he said. "After all, the most critical part of the plan has to do with you."

Celia had read the dispatch before, but now she scanned it again. Just like the first time, a flutter of apprehension passed through her as she read what would be required of her.

To A, B, C, D
From AP
A blue-ribbon USA site-selection commis-

sion of 20 officers and attached civilians is currently stationed in Denver, C.T. Its task is to select a site for a major US Army post that will be located on the eastern flank of the Rockies, anywhere from the New Mexico to Wyoming borders. The final decision is a matter of utmost secrecy. It is also a matter of intense interest to local communities, legitimate businessmen, army suppliers, and grifters and speculators. A speculator with advance knowledge of the site chosen could buy up land adjacent to it and make a killing.

The pressure on the commission to leak its verdict is enormous. At the heart of the problem is a certain Denver parlor house called Henrietta's. The place is famed for the beauty and gentility of its inmates, rich appointments, and fine food and wine. Its prices and doormen exclude all but the elite. Commission officers report a major effort by those young ladies to worm information out of the commission. The AG wishes to know who wants that information and why.

Operative A may decline this assignment. Otherwise she is to represent herself to the owner, Madam Henrietta LaBoeuf, as a lady of good breeding in need of lots of money and considering brief employment as an inmate. She is not, repeat not, to degrade herself or enter into an inmate's life. Just negotiate, seeking to learn how much money can be made fast.

Operative C will be given papers representing that he is a civilian geologist attached to the commission. If he should purchase the services of an inmate, it must be at his own expense. The army will not reimburse him from public funds.

Operative B will function as guide and assistant to Operative C in his geological expeditions. The actual goal of both operatives in this endeavor will be to discover whatever can be learned about possible corruption among commission members and/or the local citizenry. The same injunction against using public funds to purchase the services of an inmate applies as well to Operative B.

Operative D will proceed to Denver and maintain himself as inexpensively as possible while awaiting orders from Operative C. Needless to say, the same prohibitions also apply to his expenses as well.

There it was, cut and dried. Celia looked up from the dispatch as Landrum said, "Well? Do you still want to go through with it? Amos specifically said the choice was up to you."

"I said I'd do it, didn't I?" Celia replied somewhat sharply. "After all, it's not like I really have to . . . to work in that place."

His tone gentle, Glidinghawk said, Landrum and I already have an entrance into the commission, Celia. We can work the case strictly from that angle, if you'd prefer."

"No!" She was angry now. "Don't worry, I can stand to go into a high-class Denver whorehouse. After all, we were all involved in a lot worse places back in Fort Griffin."

Her words were blunt but true. This Henrietta's was probably not nearly as bad as some of the frontier dives they had seen in Texas.

Fox spoke up. "At least the three of you get to do something," he grumbled. "I'm stuck sitting in some run-down boardinghouse with barely enough money to live on. If you ask me, Colonel Powell is asking too much of us. And for God's sake, why didn't he set up a cover identity for me?"

"You're our secret weapon, Preston," Glidinghawk said. His face was serious, but there was a wry tone in his voice.

Evidently Fox didn't appreciate the humor. He continued to complain about the situation until Landrum interrupted by saying, "I'm sure there'll be something for you to do before long, Preston. Until then, just keep quiet, all right?"

Fox grimaced, but he fell silent.

Landrum turned to Celia. "When are you going to Henrietta's?"

"I thought I'd pay a visit to the place tomorrow," she replied.

"Make it tomorrow night," Landrum told her. "Gerald and I have to report to the commission tomorrow, but we should be free by nightfall. I'll make a point of being in Henrietta's myself tomorrow night."

"So you can watch out for me like a mother hen?"

The Texan grinned. "Reckon that's my job, mother hen to the strangest brood of little chicks I ever did see."

Celia had to smile back at him, her earlier resentment slipping away from her. They *were* a bunch of misfits, she supposed. A college-educated Indian, a former Confederate and Texas Ranger, an impulsive, fresh-faced lieutenant — and a young woman who had been told many times that she was too independent for her own good.

Together, though, they had learned to get results. Surely this time would not be any different.

"Is there any place around here where a young lady could get something to eat?" she asked, just a trace of sarcasm in her voice as she looked at Landrum.

"There's a restaurant in the next block," he told her. "I thought Gerald and I would stroll down there for a bite. Why don't you go first, and we'll come along a couple of minutes later. That way it won't look like we're together."

Celia nodded. "That sounds fine to me."

"And I suppose I'll have to go back to that

infernal boardinghouse and subsist on the meager fare they offer," Fox said.

"I think that's what Amos would want," Landrum told him solemnly.

Celia swallowed a laugh. She had had to live on boardinghouse food for several days during their last assignment, and she didn't envy Fox. She was sure he would survive, though.

She asked, "Is there anything else we need to cover?"

Landrum shook his head. "I think that's it for the time being. There's nothing we can decide until we've gotten more familiar with the commission and you've made your trip to Henrietta's. I've got a hunch it won't be long until things are really popping around here, though."

Celia hoped he was right. There were few things worse, in her mind, than being bored.

Well, if things got too uninteresting, she could always look up Major Devlin Henry again. That prospect made her smile.

Before this mission was over, she hoped to know the handsome major a great deal better.

# CHAPTER FOUR

The Colorado House was an imposing granite structure which almost looked more like a capitol than the capitol building did. There was a large, flagstone-paved patio in front of the hotel. The open area was surrounded by shrubbery and dotted with ornate iron poles atop which rested kerosene lamps. Several flower beds broke up the patio into smaller sections, and there were wrought iron tables and chairs here and there. In the spring and summer, it would undoubtedly be a lovely place, the kind of spot where lovers would stroll underneath the moonlight.

Now, when the sunshine was weak, the flowers were gone, and the air had a definite chill, most of the charm had deserted it.

Still, the hotel itself, rising three stories, exuded an air of solidity. It looked like the kind of place where a government commission would make its headquarters.

Landrum Davis tugged at the tie around his neck. The damned thing was threatening to cut off his air and choke him to death. He didn't know what was worse, the tie or the scratchy suit he was wearing.

Glancing at the Omaha Indian walking slightly behind him, Landrum growled a curse. Glidinghawk was one lucky son of a bitch. He got to wear his usual buckskins. He was only supposed to be a guide and assistant; he didn't have to look respectable.

Although Glidinghawk said nothing, he was well aware of Landrum's discomfiture, and while his face was typically expressionless, there was a sparkle of laughter in his dark eyes.

"What's so damned funny, redskin?" Landrum asked grouchily. "You look almost as happy as if you were scalping some poor helpless settler."

"I might point out," Glidinghawk replied, the educated tones of Dartmouth evident in his low-pitched voice, "that scalping as a custom originated with the white man. French fur trappers, to be precise. The Indians have always gotten an inordinate amount of blame for starting a practice that is barbaric at best."

"Oh, shut up," Landrum said.

"Injun be heap quiet, boss."

Landrum gritted his teeth and led the way across the patio, up a couple of steps, and through the massive double doors of the hotel's entrance.

Just inside the lobby, a burly man in a long red coat and a cap raised a hand to stop them. "Excuse me, sir," he said to Landrum. "I'm afraid the hotel doesn't allow Indians on the premises."

Landrum glanced coldly at him. "You some kind of doorman?"

"I suppose you could call me that, sir. If you'd care to have your servant wait outside . . . I assume he is your servant—"

"No, he's my long-lost daddy," Landrum snapped. As an angry expression began to form on the doorman's face, Landrum sighed and raised a hand. "I'm sorry, mister. I had no call to jump on you. My name's Landrum Davis, and I'm here to report to the U.S. Army commission as a civilian geologist. This Indian is my assistant, and I really need him to stay with me."

The commission obviously carried a lot of weight around here. The doorman's officious attitude immediately vanished. He said, "In that case, sir, you just go right on up. The commission has the entire third floor booked. They're using the suite at the head of the stairs as their office." The doorman lowered his voice slightly as he went on, "There'll be sentries up there, and they may not be as tolerant of the Indian as I am."

"I'll set them straight," Landrum assured the man. As he and Glidinghawk started across the lobby, they exchanged a mutual look of disgust.

41

Landrum could understand a white man's prejudice against Indians. He had felt it himself at times — before meeting Gerald Glidinghawk. Since that time he and the Omaha had become fast friends. Landrum had learned a great deal about Indians, and he realized now that the redskin problem was not one with clear-cut answers.

He also knew about the military, had in fact learned a lot about how it operated since going to work for Amos Powell. And sometimes it was a wonder that the army ever got anything accomplished.

He guessed the real reason he was so touchy this morning was all this pretending to be something he wasn't. That was all part of being an undercover agent, but sometimes it was harder than others.

Like when the role he was playing required him to wear a damned tie!

"I've been meaning to ask you," Glidinghawk said as they started up the broad staircase, "how much do you know about geology anyway?" The Omaha spoke in a low voice that could not have been overheard more than a couple of feet away.

"Not a whole hell of a lot," Landrum replied. "I know a few different kinds of rocks when I see 'em, but that's about it."

Glidinghawk nodded. "It's a good thing I took several courses in the subject back at the university. Perhaps we can fake our way through that part of the assignment."

"Yeah. Lucky."

As the doorman had said, there were sentries posted at the top of the stairs where the third-floor landing opened up. The two young privates stiffened to alertness as Landrum and Gliding-hawk approached. One of them said to Landrum, "That's far enough, sir. Please state your business."

"This isn't a fort, son," Landrum told him.

"No, sir, but as long as the commission is staying here, it is a military installation. Now, if you please, tell us why you're here."

Landrum saw the way they tightly gripped the carbines in their hands. There was something bizarre—something *wrong*—about this whole situation. The tension in the atmosphere was enough to tell him that the commission had had plenty of trouble since arriving in Denver.

Moving slowly so as not to spook the guards, Landrum reached inside his coat and brought out the envelope containing his identification papers and the dummied-up orders that had brought him here.

"My name is Landrum Davis," he said. "I'm a geologist, and I've been hired to work with the commission." He made a show of glancing at the orders. "I'm supposed to report to a Colonel Matthias Porter."

"Yes, sir," the young sentry replied briskly. "What about the Indian, sir?"

"He's my guide and assistant. I'll take the responsibility for him."

"Very good, sir. Could I see those orders?"

Landrum handed over the phony documents. Of course, they were phony only in that they misrepresented him and his mission. They had been prepared by Amos Powell and were authentic in every other way.

"Very good, sir," the sentry repeated, handing back the papers. "If you'll follow me . . ."

Landrum and Glidinghawk fell in behind the private. He led them the few feet to the doors of the suite that the commission was using as its office. A sharp rap on the panel brought a muffled command to come in. The sentry opened one of the doors and stepped back to allow Landrum and Glidinghawk to enter.

Inside the big sitting room of the suite, the normal hotel furnishings had been replaced with desks and tables and straight-backed chairs. There were topographical maps tacked to the walls instead of the scenic chromolithographs that usually decorated such rooms. Several officers were sitting at the desks, paperwork scattered in front of them. At a long table, two men stood poring over an unrolled map. One of them wore the uniform of a full colonel and boer a resemblance to President Grant during his Civil War days; the colonel was taller and brawnier than Grant had ever been, however. The other man was a well-dressed civilian, a silver-haired man with muttonchop whiskers and a full mustache.

The colonel glanced up and, around a big cigar that was also reminiscent of U. S. Grant, grunted, "What can I do for you, mister?" His eyes narrowed as he spotted Glidinghawk behind Landrum.

The Texan extended his hand. Damned if he was going to salute. "I'm Landrum Davis," he said. "I'm supposed to report to Colonel Porter."

"I'm Porter," the officer said, shaking hands briefly. "Let's see your papers."

Landrum passed them across the table to Porter, who scanned them and handed them back. The colonel nodded to the civilian. "This is Mr. Rainsford, the commission's top civilian. You'll be working primarily for him, Davis."

Landrum shook hands with the civilian, who said. "Tom Rainsford, Mr. Davis. You'd be the geologist we've been expecting, am I right?"

"That's right, sir," Landrum replied.

"Who the devil's the Indian?" Colonel Porter asked.

Before Landrum could answer, the Omaha thumped his chest with a closed fist and said gutturally, "Me Glidinghawk. Best damn guide and scout on all of frontier, you betcha."

Landrum bit back a curse and tried not to roll his eyes.

"Keep your mouth shut, redskin," he said. "Your job is to tote my equipment and show me around, not to talk."

Glidinghawk nodded solemnly. Landrum knew

damn well the Indian was laughing at him again. One of these days he was going to have boot the Omaha's red ass but good. Who needed an educated Indian with such a perverted sense of humor?

Well, right now he needed Glidinghawk, Landrum thought in answer to his own question.

"Do you know what the purpose of this commission is, Davis," Porter was asking now.

"Well, sir, not really," Landrum replied with a shake of his head. "All I know for sure is that you're interested in getting some geological surveys of certain areas."

Porter nodded. "That's right. And that's all you need to know. Rainsford here is our chief surveyor. I'll turn you over to him." Porter scooped up his hat from the table and settled it on his grizzled head. "I'll be back later, Mr. Rainsford. Why don't you give Davis his orders?"

"Of course, Colonel." As Porter stalked out of the big room, Rainsford turned the map on the table around and moved it closer to Landrum and Glidinghawk. "You see these areas marked in red, Landrum? You don't mind if I call you Landrum, do you?"

"That's fine," Landrum replied. He put a blunt finger on one of the areas marked on the map. "These the places you want me to look over?"

Rainsford nodded. "That's right. We need to know the geological makeup of the areas. We would also like your opinion on how construction would fare in these vicinities."

Landrum looked at him shrewdly. "This wouldn't have anything to do with some new fort the army's thinking of building, would it?"

He had carefully considered the question of whether he should reveal that he knew the purpose of the commission. As many rumors as were floating around Denver, according to Amos Powell, it made sense that he would have at least heard the speculation about a new fort. To plead too much ignorance would be a mistake, Landrum had decided.

Rainsford smiled. "I see you know a bit more than you told the good colonel. It's probably wise that you didn't let on any more than you did with him. He is a bit overly fond of military secrecy." The civilian kept his voice pitched low, so that the other officers in the room wouldn't overhear his words.

Landrum studied the map and the marked areas again. Several of them were close to Denver, while others were as far away as New Mexico and Wyoming. "I'll start with these nearby," he said, stabbing one of them with a finger, "then work my way out. That way you'll at least have some of my reports quickly."

That decision also meant that he could stay in the Denver area. He wouldn't be doing the investigation any good if he and Glidinghawk were way the hell up and gone in Wyoming.

"Excellent idea," Rainsford replied. "Can you

get started right away?"

"Tomorrow," Landrum replied. "I'll need to pick up some supplies and get outfitted today. But we can set out first thing in the morning."

"Very good." Rainsford came out from behind the table and walked with Landrum and Glidinghawk to the door of the suite. Landrum sensed that the man had something else to say, and when they had reached the hall, Rainsford went on in a quiet voice, "I can't emphasize enough the need for caution, Landrum. Despite what I said earlier about Colonel Porter, there is a legitimate need for secrecy in the commission's activities. That's why you are to report only to the colonel or myself. Don't turn any maps or drawings or reports over to anyone else, understand?"

Landrum nodded. "Of course, Mr. Rainsford."

"What about the Indian? Is he trustworthy?"

Landrum glanced at Glidinghawk's impassive face. In a whisper, he replied, "He's not really bright enough to be a danger to anyone, sir."

Rainsford nodded. "Very good. We're relying on you, Landrum. Don't let us down."

"I won't," the Texan promised.

He shook hands with Rainsford again, then went past the sentries and started down the stairs, Glidinghawk at his heels. When they were out of earshot of the young troopers, the Omaha said, "I suppose I deserved that little comment."

"Damn right you did," Landrum growled. "You've been riding me all morning, you blamed heathen." He tugged at the uncomfortable collar and tie again. "I'll be glad when we can get out of town and dress like normal folks again."

"What's normal?"

"Don't get all philosophic on me, dammit. It sure as hell ain't this."

When they had left the hotel, Glidinghawk asked, "Do you want me to see about getting horses and supplies?"

"I guess so," Landrum answered. "We're going to have to at least look like we're doing our job with the commission. I want to keep these little expeditions as short as possible, though. Celia's liable to need us in town."

That reminded him of the planned trip to Madam Henrietta's parlor house tonight. Celia would be making her first contact, her first visit to the place where the trouble seemed to be centered.

Landrum hoped that everything went well.

Considering the way things usually went for Powell's Army, in this case good luck might well mean that nobody would get killed.

# CHAPTER FIVE

Celia Louise Burnett felt her heart fluttering as she stepped down from the carriage she had hired to bring her to Henrietta's. She was nervous, but she was determined to swallow her anxiety and proceed with the mission as planned.

"Are you sure this is where you wanted to go, miss?" the carriage's driver asked as he leaned over from his seat.

"Yes, I'm sure," Celia replied, her voice steadier than she really felt. She reached inside her bag and brought out a bill. Handing it up to the driver, she asked, "How difficult is it to find a carriage for hire along this street at night?"

The man laughed shortly. "On this block, not hard at all, lady. I'm probably doing myself out of some extra money by telling you that, but there's no need to hire me to wait, if that's what you're getting at."

"Thank you. That is exactly what I was getting at."

She passed another bill up to him. "I'd like for you to wait anyway."

The driver took the money and grinned down at her in the light of a nearby streetlamp. "Much obliged, miss. I'll be out here when you're ready to leave."

Celia nodded and turned away from the carriage.

The house was large and well lit, sitting behind a tall fence and a big yard on a broad street lined with trees. This was a highly respectable neighborhood, and Celia's destination looked more like the sort of mansion a wealthy businessman would build for his wife, rather than the most expensive and exclusive house of pleasure in the city.

The driver had been very dubious when she had hired his carriage in front of the hotel and told him where she was going. She had been forced to reassure him several times that she knew what she was doing and knew what kind of place Henrietta's was.

"All right, miss," he had finally said. "It's just that I don't recollect ever taking anyone except gentlemen there."

"Then I'm an exception to the rule," Celia had told him. It was only after she was settled in the carriage that she had blushed with the sudden realization the driver might think she was the sort of warped woman who was interested in other females.

Of course, she couldn't very well tell him that she was visiting Henrietta's to inquire about the possibility of employment. She didn't have to tell him anything. It was none of his business, and she shouldn't feel compelled to explain herself.

Now that she was here, there was nothing left to do but square her shoulders and go on in.

The gate in the fence was unlocked. She opened it and went through it into the yard. A walk paved with stones led up to the house, which loomed large in the early evening shadows. It had several stories, and a long veranda ran along the entire front of it.

Celia went up several steps onto the veranda. A lantern hung over the double doors leading into the house. The doors were thick panels of wood on the bottom, ornately engraved glass on the top. Such doors had to be expensive and were probably shipped out from the East somewhere.

Celia was just reaching out to grasp the highly polished brass knob of the right-hand door when it abruptly swung open. A man started through it, heading out, and nearly barged right into her. Celia stepped back quickly and could not stifle a gasp of surprise.

The man stopped in his tracks, equally shocked that he had nearly run into a very attractive young redhead. As he settled a fancy bowler hat on his carefully barbered head, a confident smile stretched across his wide face.

"Well, well, well," he boomed. "What have we here? My sincerest apologies, my dear. I didn't mean to nearly trample you like a bull buffalo!"

Celia smiled weakly. "That's quite all right, sir. I should have been more careful about watching where I'm going."

"Not that a collision would have been entirely unpleasant, eh?" the man smirked. "Are you one of Madam Henrietta's new employees?"

Celia forced her smile to become saucier. "I hope to be," she said bluntly.

The man moved to take her arm. "Well, come in, come in. Henrietta and I are old friends. In apology for nearly running you down, I shall give you my personal recommendation. How's that?"

"Why, thank you, sir." Celia wanted to shrink from the man's touch, but she controlled the impulse.

"Of course," the man said, lowering his voice and leaning closer to her so that his arm pressed against the side of her breast, "I shall want to confirm for myself later on that my recommendation was warranted."

"Of course," Celia murmured.

What would Amos Powell think of her now, Celia wondered. His orders had specifically said that she was not to degrade herself, and here she was making arrangements to sell her favors later on to a perfect stranger. She didn't intend to follow through on the situation, but still, Amos would probably be scandalized. She knew Preston

Fox would be, despite the fact that he himself had become romantically involved with a prostitute on their last mission.

"My name is Warren Judson," the man in the bowler hat was saying to her now as they entered the building. He swept the hat back off and led Celia into a foyer. Two large men in expensive suits stood there.

"Back so soon, Mr. Judson?" one of them asked. Neither of the men looked overly bright, but they exuded strength. No doubt their job was to greet guests and keep the riffraff out.

"This young lady and I have some business to discuss with Madam LaBoeuf," Judson said. "I assume she is up in her suite?"

"Yes, sir," the other doorman answered. He, like his companion, was staring curiously at Celia. "If you and the young lady would care to wait at the bar, I'll inform Madam that you wish to see her."

"Thank you, Carl," Judson said solemnly. To Celia, he said, "Come along, my dear."

As they left the foyer and entered a large parlor, Celia reflected that she had been lucky to have almost run into Judson. The man was obviously important and wielded some influence here, and with his assistance she was going to be able to see Madam Henrietta almost immediately.

The sights and sounds of the parlor were enough to take Celia's breath away and distract her thoughts from the plan she and the others had worked out.

The room was large and high-ceilinged, and sparkling crystal chandeliers cast a warm glow over the merrymakers who filled the parlor. There were high-backed armchairs and low, heavy sofas arranged around the room, and at the far end was an open space where several couples danced to the music provided by a group of musicians on a low bandstand.

There were more women than men in the room, but the mix was fairly even. The men were all prosperous-looking, sporting fine suits and pomaded hair. The women were all young and beautiful, dressed in stylish gowns with necklines that plunged daringly. Black waiters in tight red jackets circulated through the room bearing trays of drinks brought from a long mahogany bar on the other side of the parlor. An arched doorway led on into another room, this one full of tables where couples dined on food that looked delicious.

A pleasant mixture of conversation and laughter filled the air. The women were all smiling and laughing, Celia saw, evidently having the best time of their lives. Perhaps it was all a sham, but the men dancing and talking with the women didn't seem to mind. They gratefully accepted the pretense of elegance and glamour and romance.

And perhaps it was not all pretense. Madam Henrietta's looked like a much nicer place to ply this particular trade than any Celia had ever seen.

It was infinitely better than the pigpens of Dodge City and Fort Griffin. A girl could do much worse for herself out here on the frontier.

Warren Judson led the way across the crowded parlor to the bar. Celia felt herself the object of several stares along the way. The men in the room were looking at her in frank appreciation. Her suit was cut much more modestly than the gowns worn by the inmates, but it did nothing to conceal her lush red hair, worn up on her head in an intricate pile of curls, on her equally impressive curves.

The women watching her were simply jealous, Celia told herself.

"Well, my dear, what would you like to drink?" Judson asked when they reached the bar.

Celia would have liked a glass of bourbon, but brandy was more in keeping with the image she was trying to project. "Perhaps some cognac," she said to Judson with a smile.

"Very good." He boomed the order to one of the red-jacketed bartenders, who brought two snifters of the liquor.

The glasses held more brandy than Celia really wanted. She knew she had to keep her wits about her this evening. But it would look strange if she did not drink, and she didn't want to draw any extra attention to herself.

She picked up the large snifter nearest her and raised it slowly. Judson lifted his and clinked it against hers. "To fortunate meetings," he said.

"To fortunate meetings," Celia echoed.

She sipped the brandy and let her eyes roam around the crowded room. She had seen no sign of Landrum Davis yet, and he had said he would be here tonight. In fact, she had seen him at the hotel earlier, and he had set out for Henrietta's first. He should have already been here.

Celia wondered suddenly if he was upstairs with one of the women. She had already seen several couples going up and down the broad, curving staircase that led to the upper floors. There seemed to be a steady traffic to that area of the house.

"Excellent brandy, eh?" Judson asked, breaking into Celia's train of thought.

"What? Oh, yes, indeed. Excellent."

That would be just like Landrum, she thought. He was all business most of the time, but when he got a little too much to drink, or when he decided he was old and lonely, his professionalism slipped. When you got right down to it, for all their fancy dress and manners, these women were whores—and Landrum had a soft spot for whores.

Whether he was here or not, Celia would have to go through with her part of the operation. She was already on the verge of accomplishing her first goal; this was no time to worry or back out.

She suddenly felt Judson's big hand on her body. He had moved closer to her and put his snifter back on the bar, and now he had that hand on her back, pressing gently but insistently against her firm flesh. Instinctively, she stiffened.

"Madam Henrietta certainly knows how to make a man feel at home," he said softly. "You'd do well to remember that, my dear, if you wish to work for her." His tone was gently chiding.

Celia made herself nod and relax. "Yes. You're right, Mr. Judson."

"Call me Warren. And you haven't told me your name," he reminded her.

"Of course. I'm so forgetful. I'm Celia Burnett . . . Warren."

"Very pleased to meet you, Miss Celia Burnett." Judson's hand moved up her back toward her shoulders, the fingers moving in a sensuous massage. Suddenly, his fingers dipped down toward the flare of her hips. This time she managed not to flinch. The smile on her lips didn't waver.

If she had to let this man paw her to get the job done . . . Well, there were worse things. As she looked more closely at what was going on in the parlor on the long sofas, she saw that indeed worse things were going on right under her nose.

Suddenly, she spotted a familiar face. A lean man in a white coat was moving through the crowd. The last time she had seen Oliver Blaine had been on the train coming into Denver the night before. Evidently the gambler had decided to stay in town for a while.

Celia hoped Blaine wouldn't notice her. He might speak to her, and she didn't want to have to explain to Judson or Madam Henrietta why she had been involved in a poker game and a shooting on the train. She was supposed to be a well-bred young lady who was unfortunately down on her luck at the moment. She didn't want the madam knowing that she was actually less innocent than she seemed.

Blaine moved on, taking a deck of cards from his pocket and riffling the pasteboards. He stopped and spoke to several men along the way, and a few of them joined him. Together, the small group went through the dining room and exited through a door in the far wall. Evidently Blaine was getting another game started.

A man came down the staircase alone. He wore a plain suit and had a thin face and pale hair. Round, rimless spectacles made his blue eyes seem larger than they really were. He wove through the crowd skillfully and came up to Judson and Celia.

"Good evening, Mr. Judson," the man said in a soft voice. "Madam LaBoeuf had a message that you wished to see her."

"That's right, Roland," Judson replied. He squeezed Celia's arm. "I want to introduce this young lady to her."

The man called Roland let his gaze play over Celia for an instant. His eyes were intense, and Celia felt as if he had seen everything there was to see about her in that brief glance.

For a split second, she had even felt naked

under that gaze.

Then Roland nodded. "Yes, indeed," he said slowly. "I believe that Henrietta will certainly want to meet the young lady. If you'll come with me, please."

He preceded them across the room, moving with an easy grace. There was something slightly dangerous about him. Judson seemed massive and clumsy next to Roland's slim menace.

The three of them ascended the staircase. At the second-floor landing, Roland started down a long hall. The corridor was lined with oil paintings and reminded Celia more of a museum than a parlor house. Roland stopped in front of a heavy wooden door and rapped lightly on it.

"Come in," a female voice called from inside.

Roland opened the door and held it for Celia and Judson. Celia felt a momentary surge of trepidation. She wanted to cut and run and say the hell with Amos Powell and his assignments.

But then the professional within her took over, and she willed her steps to carry her into the room. Judson's firm grip on her arm made it impossible for her to do anything else.

She stepped into a room that was part office, part sitting room. A huge desk took up most of the space on the right side of the room, and a beautiful woman with brunette hair sat behind the desk.

The left side of the room was furnished with another of the long, low, heavy sofas, and a man in a blue uniform was sitting there, his attitude casual. He stiffened suddenly, sitting upright, and his jaw tightened as his eyes met Celia's.

She wondered, her head suddenly spinning dizzily, what Major Devlin Henry was doing here.

# CHAPTER SIX

Madam Henrietta LaBoeuf laced slim fingers together and rested her chin on them, smiling slightly at Celia. To Judson, she said, "Why, Warren, who's your little friend? She's quite lovely."

Celia tried to keep her breathing under control as she forced her eyes away from Devlin's. Working as an undercover agent had given her plenty of opportunity to polish her natural acting skills, and she needed all of them now to cover up her surprise.

Judson said, "Henrietta, allow me to present Miss Celia Burnett. Celia, this is Madam Henrietta LaBoeuf."

"I'm very pleased to meet you, Celia," Henrietta said in her throaty voice. "What brings you to our little establishment?"

"I'm pleased to meet you, ma'am." Celia's voice was much stronger and calmer than she had expected it to be, giving the tightness of her throat and the state of her nerves. "I've heard a great deal about you."

Celia regretted her choice of words as Judson laughed boomingly. "And most of it true, I'll wager," he said heartily.

"I . . . I didn't mean—" Celia began haltingly.

Henrietta waved a beautifully manicured hand. "Don't worry about it, my dear. When one is something of a celebrity, one must get used to the fact that people talk. Now, why are you here?"

Celia glanced at Devlin, who had not spoken so far. He seemed to be totally absorbed in the pattern of the wallpaper. Celia sensed that he didn't want her saying anything about the fact that they knew each other.

That was fine with her. She had no idea why Devlin was here, but whatever the reason, it was none of her business.

Abruptly, she realized that there might be a very good reason for him to be visiting Madam Henrietta. He might be here as a customer, of course.

For some reason, Celia felt a surge of resentment at that thought. It had never occurred to her that Devlin might be the kind of man who would patronize such an establishment. He was young and virile, though. Like all men, he would have needs that must be met.

But women had needs, too, and Celia realized

she had begun thinking of Devlin Henry as the kind of man who might meet some of hers.

Henrietta was waiting for an answer to her question. Celia smiled again, and said, "I would like to discuss a business matter with you, ma'am. If I could talk to you in private . . ."

"Don't worry about the major, darling. He's an old friend. Aren't you, Devlin?"

"Of course," Devlin replied smoothly. He stood up and went on, "But I have to be leaving anyway. It was nice seeing you again, Henrietta." He took the hand she extended to him and lifted it to his lips for a moment. Then he turned to Celia, nodded, and left through the door, clutching his hat in his hands.

"Such a dear boy," Henrietta purred, gazing after him. She switched her attention back to Celia. "Now, Miss Burnett, I believe you were going to tell me why you've come to my house. Pay no mind to Warren here. He is an old and valued advisor, as well as a customer, and Roland is my right hand. He's privy to everything to do with the house. So you can speak in front of them."

"Very well." Celia felt better now that Devlin was gone. She was sure from the way he had acted that he had come to Madam Henrietta's as a customer. Since he had never been to Denver before, he must have known her from somewhere else and, hearing that she was in business here, looked her up to renew acquaintances. That clear in her mind, Celia went on, "I've come to see about the possibility of employment, ma'am."

Henrietta's smile became more smug. "That doesn't surprise me, Miss Burnett, but I must say I'm pleased. As soon as you came in I thought to myself that here was a lovely girl." Her voice became harder. "Just one thing before we continue this discussion. Don't call me ma'am. I'm not *that* much older than you, dear."

That was true enough. Celia put Henrietta's age in the late twenties or early thirties. There appeared to be no gray at all in her thick, luxuriant hair. It was a rich brunette shade that went well with her lightly tanned skin. She was undeniably lovely, although Celia could see cunning and a certain hardness in her brown eyes.

"All right," Celia said. "What shall I call you?"

"How about Henrietta? It is my name. My actual name, I might add. Unlike some women in my line of work, I've never felt compelled to change it." She looked shrewdly at Celia. "You do know what my line of work is, don't you, Celia?"

The young redhead nodded and licked her lips. "I know," she said. "I'm not quite as . . . unworldly as I might appear, Henrietta."

"Excellent! A certain amount of experience always comes in helpful."

Celia let herself sound slightly offended. "I am

a young lady of good breeding, however," she said stiffly.

"Relax, Celia," Warren Judson told her. "No one has said otherwise, have they?"

"Well . . . no."

Henrietta leaned forward. "All of my young ladies are quite genteel, Celia. I daresay you won't find a more elegant group of girls anywhere west of the Mississippi. Or east of it, for that matter." She waved a hand at their opulent surroundings. "A place like this requires a great deal of money to operate. Therefore our prices might seem, to some, to be exorbitant. But I promise you, we deliver value for value received. My young ladies are beautiful and well mannered. The cream of the crop, so to speak. And now you wish to join them."

"I . . . I had that in mind," Celia admitted. "I'm rather financially embarrassed at the moment, and I'd rather my family not know about my problems. You understand."

"Of course." Henrietta glanced at the two men. "What do you gentlemen think? Should I offer Miss Burnett an opportunity to reverse her fortunes?"

As the gazes of Judson and Roland played over her again, Celia tried to keep the smile on her face and not allow the groan she felt to escape her throat. This was all going too fast! Madam Henrietta was about to offer her a job here at the parlor house, and this first visit had been intended only to test the waters. What was she going to do?

She wished she could talk to Landrum or Glidinghawk.

But she was on her own, and the choice would have to be hers.

"Indeed," Judson murmured. "I think it would be a fine idea to employ Miss Burnett, Henrietta. I told her downstairs that I would give her my personal recommendation, and so I shall. And as your banker, I think it would be a wise business move as well."

Henrietta cocked an eyebrow inquiringly. "Oh? Are you and the young lady already, ah, acquainted, Warren?"

"Not in the way you mean. I hope to be shortly, however," Judson answered bluntly.

"And what about your opinion, Roland?"

The slim man moved in front of Celia, still looking her over intently. Again she felt the sinisterness that seemed to ooze from him, and it was all she could do to keep the pleasant expression plastered on her face. She was suddenly as frightened as she had ever been.

Finally, Roland slowly bobbed his head up and down. "She'll do," he announced flatly.

Henrietta stood up behind the desk. "Well, my dear, that leaves it up to you, doesn't it?"

"What sort of financial arrangement would we

have?" Celia asked.

"The house sets the fees and takes half," Henrietta answered, her tone businesslike. "In case you didn't know it, that's very generous. Most places take a lot more than half."

"Yes," Celia murmured, "very generous. But I . . . I may have need of a great deal of money."

"What you earn depends on how hard you work." Henrietta looked speculatively at her. "And what you're willing to do."

"I'm . . . willing to do almost anything," Celia said boldly.

"Then I'd say you'll do quite well. Do we have an agreement?"

Celia steeled herself. The situation had gotten out of hand, but that didn't mean she had to let herself be carried along in its flow. She said, "I mean no offense, but I would like to think about it first."

Henrietta shrugged. "That's up to you, but I can promise you that you won't find a better deal anywhere in Denver."

Judson leaned closer to Celia and said in a stage whisper, "I'd jump at the chance if I were you, Miss Burnett."

"I . . . I really have to think about it."

"Whatever you wish," Henrietta said sweetly. Celia thought she saw a hint of disappointment in the older woman's eyes, though. Henrietta went on, "I've enjoyed talking to you, Celia. Why don't

I have Roland show you out the back way? That will be easier."

And it would keep Celia from distracting any of the customers in the parlor again, she thought. Celia was not happy about being turned over to Roland, but surely nothing would happen right here in the house.

"Thank you," she said, extending her hand to Henrietta. "I'll be in touch with you."

"I hope so," Henrietta replied, returning the handshake. "I'd like to see you working here, Celia."

Celia took a deep breath. "I have a feeling you will."

Roland took her arm. She let him turn her toward the door, and as the slim man opened it, she heard Henrietta say, "Stay for a few minutes, will you, Warren? There are some other matters I want to discuss with you."

"Of course, my dear," Judson replied.

Roland closed the door behind them, cutting off the conversation. Celia glanced at him nervously, hoping he would not want an advance sample of the merchandise Madam Henrietta hoped to be selling.

He seemed rather detached, however, and showed little interest in her as he led her down a rear staircase and showed her to a side entrance. "Do you have a carriage waiting?" he asked. "If you don't, I can summon one for you?"

"Thank you," Celia replied. "My driver promised to wait for me, so I'm sure I'll be all right."

There was sudden commotion behind Roland in the corridor leading to the side door. Two men of the same sort as the burly doormen appeared, holding a struggling figure between them. As they dragged him toward the door, the man yelled, "You can't do this to me, you bastards! I ain't drunk! Ain't never been drunk in my life!"

The man's slurred speech and staggering walk testified differently, however. He appeared to be as drunk as a lord.

Celia flinched.

Roland saw the reaction and took her arm, gently moving her out of the way as the bouncers hauled the sot out of the house and past them. "Don't worry," Roland assured her. "Things like this happen—men often have too much to drink—but it's nothing to concern yourself with. Our men are well trained and quite capable of handling any problems. And they're never more than a moment away while you're in the house."

Celia nodded somewhat shakily. She watched as the husky employees took the man through the small garden at the side of the house and deposited him somewhat roughly on the street. They walked back toward the house, brushing their hands off, as the drunk slowly and unsteadily raised himself onto all fours. He climbed groggily to his feet and staggered off, singing softly to himself and disappearing in a patch of shadow.

Roland shook his head. "Disgraceful," he muttered, in the strongest expression of opinion that Celia had yet heard from him.

"Yes," she agreed.

It sure as hell was disgraceful, and the next time she saw Landrum Davis, she was going to have a few things to say to him about this disgusting performance.

# CHAPTER SEVEN

Celia was furious by the time she got back to her hotel. Landrum had insisted on being at Madam Henrietta's at the same time she was, and then he had gotten stinking drunk! He would have been a great help if she had wound up in trouble, Celia thought bitterly.

The clerk gave her a surprised look as she came through the lobby with a stormy expression on her face, but Celia paid no attention to him. She went up the stairs, anxious to get back to her room and think over everything that had happened. She should find Glidinghawk and tell him about Landrum, she knew, but at the moment, she just wasn't in the mood.

Celia took the key to her room from her bag and unlocked the door. The hall was deserted at the moment. As she turned the knob and began to open the door, it was suddenly jerked out of her hand.

Gasping in surprise, Celia automatically pulled back slightly. A figure came barreling out of the room. Celia had time to see that it was a man with a slouch hat pulled down over his eyes, concealing much of his face, before he slammed into her with his shoulder and sent her reeling.

She staggered backward. Her head cracked sharply against the opposite wall of the hall. Her vision blurred for a moment, and then as it cleared, she saw the intruder running down the hall toward the staircase.

Celia's hand dove into her bag, the fingers closing around the butt of the two-shot derringer she carried there. As she pulled the little gun out and started to lift it, another man suddenly appeared in front of the fleeing stranger.

Landrum Davis took in the scene—Celia down the hall in front of her door, a gun in her hand, and a strange man dashing away from her—and reacted immediately. As he reached the top of the stairs, he dove forward, throwing himself in front of the running man.

The intruder couldn't stop in time. His legs hit Landrum's body. His balance gone, the man pinwheeled forward, over Landrum's back, to smash heavily against the floor of the landing.

Landrum rolled and came up reaching for his Colt .44. He yanked the gun from its holster and lined it on the stranger, earing back the hammer and barking, "Hold it!" He heard Celia's rapid footsteps as she hurried down the hall to join him.

Celia kept her derringer out and ready as she came up beside Landrum. He didn't appear drunk at all now. In fact, to judge from the way he had handled the intruder, he was stone cold sober. The barrel of his .44 didn't waver as he covered the man.

Landrum flicked a gaze at Celia and said in a voice loud enough to be heard downstairs by the clerk, "What happened, ma'am? Was this varmint bothering you?"

Celia was glad he had the presence of mind to try to preserve their cover identities. She said, "He . . . he was in my room. He must be a thief. I was so frightened—" She didn't have to try very hard to make her voice sound shaky.

Landrum glanced meaningfully at the derringer, and Celia stuffed it back in her bag just as the clerk came out from behind his desk and started up the stairs. "What's wrong?" the clerk asked anxiously as he saw the gun in Landrum's steady hand.

Landrum nodded toward the stranger. "I was just going up to my room when I saw this fella running away from the lady. She says he broke into her room."

The clerk paled. He turned to Celia. "I assure you, Miss Burnett, this is a respectable hotel. We never have trouble like this. I'll summon the authorities immediately."

Celia didn't much like the idea of getting the local police involved, since that might draw more attention to her than she wanted, but she didn't see any way out of it. The clerk would certainly be suspicious if she told him not to bother.

"Thank you," she said. "I had better check to see if he stole anything from my room."

"Good idea," Landrum grunted.

Celia hurried down the hall to her room and went inside. The lamp was lit, and she could tell in its glow that while the room had been searched, nothing appeared to be missing.

A shiver went down her back. A sneak thief would have taken *something*. Was it possible that someone suspected she was hiding something and had sent the man here to try to discover her secrets? Could Madam Henrietta be behind this? She would have had to work quickly if she was, because Celia had only left the parlor house a short time earlier.

She rejoined Landrum in the hall. The clerk was gone, no doubt to find a deputy. The intruder had moved into a sitting position, his back leaned against the wall. His hat had come off in his fall, revealing a thin, beard-stubbled face. His head was hanging dejectedly now. He was making no attempt to explain or defend his actions.

"Nothing is missing, sir," she said to Landrum. "I must have interrupted the man before he had a chance to steal anything."

As Landrum glanced at her, she gave an almost

unnoticable shake of her head to let him know that there was more to this than a simple aborted robbery.

There had been no time to wonder about his changed demeanor, but now Celia began to speculate that perhaps she had been too hasty in judging him. It was possible, she suddenly realized, that he hadn't been drunk at Madam Henrietta's at all. The whole business could have been a pose.

After all, he had been nearby when Roland was escorting her out of the place, and for all she knew, he could have stayed close once he was concealed in the shadows after having been dumped in the street.

He could have been keeping an eye on her all along.

Well, she thought, slightly mollified, the least he could do would be to tell her his plans next time, so that she wouldn't think he was such a besotted lowlife.

"The clerk should be back in a few minutes with a badge toter," Landrum said. "Until then, ma'am, with your permission, I'd like to ask this man some questions."

"By all means," Celia replied. "Go right ahead."

Landrum prodded the man's leg with a boot. "Look at me, mister."

The man raised his head slowly. His gaze was stubborn and hostile.

"What the devil were you doing in the lady's room?" Landrum demanded.

"Go to hell," the man shot back.

Landrum kicked him.

Celia couldn't repress a gasp as the toe of Landrum's boot thudded into the man's thigh. The man let out a yelp of pain and grasped his leg with both hands.

"I'll go after ribs next," Landrum said stonily. "After that . . . well, let's just say you'd better talk now while you've got the chance."

The man gritted his teeth against the pain and said, "I ain't tellin' you a damn thing. You're no lawman."

Landrum tensed to launch another kick, but Celia caught his arm. "Really, sir, that's not necessary. Nothing was taken."

The intruder's eyes were downcast again, so Landrum met Celia's gaze and shook his head quickly. There was a warning look on his face, and Celia knew he wanted her to stay out of this.

She wasn't going to stand by and let him assault the man, though. No matter what he had done, that just wasn't in her makeup. She went on, "The law can handle this."

"All right," Landrum growled. "Let the law handle it. But you're making a mistake."

Celia just shook her head.

The door of the lobby opened and the clerk came in, followed closely by a thick-waisted man in a suit and Stetson. The man had a star on his coat. They hurried up the stairs, and the clerk said, "There he is, Deputy. That man there is the thief."

The deputy reached down, caught the intruder by the arm, and hauled him to his feet. "All right, you, come along." He glanced over at Celia. "You do want to press charges, don't you, ma'am?"

Celia's head was aching where she had struck it against the wall, and she could already tell that there would be a bruise on her side where the man had run into her. "Yes," she said firmly. "I want him locked up."

Vindictiveness wasn't the only thing that motivated her decision to press charges. As far as she knew, there was nothing in her room that the man could have discovered to compromise her cover identity, but just in case he had found something suspicious, she wanted him out of circulation for a while.

"I've seen this fella around town before," the deputy said. "He's probably wanted a few other places. We'll check him out, ma'am. You'll have to come down to the sheriff's office sometime and sign a complaint."

"Will tomorrow be all right for that?" Celia asked.

"That'll be fine." The deputy started down the stairs with the would-be burglar in tow, the man's thin body looking even more frail next to the lawman's burly figure.

Landrum had holstered his gun. The clerk was still standing on the stairs, so when Landrum turned toward Celia, he asked, "Are you sure you're all right, ma'am?"

"I'm fine," she replied. "Just a bit shaken up. Thank you for your help, sir."

Landrum retrieved his hat from the floor and put it on, touching the brim and nodding to her. "Landrum Davis, at your service, ma'am."

"I'm Celia Burnett." She extended her hand to him.

He continued the pretense, taking her hand and saying, "Glad to meet you, Miss Burnett. If I can be of any further assistance . . ."

"I'll be sure to let you know, Mr. Davis. Thank you again."

The clerk spoke up. "I hope you won't hold this against the hotel, Miss Burnett. Like I said, we just don't have this kind of trouble—"

"You did tonight, sonny," Landrum cut in. "I reckon you'd better keep a closer eye on the folks coming and going around here."

The clerk bobbed his head. "I will, sir. You can bet on that." With a nervous smile, he went back down the stairs to his post behind the desk.

"Well . . . good night, Mr. Davis," Celia said, still loud enough for the clerk to hear.

"Good night, ma'am."

They went to their rooms, and each of them shut their doors firmly and audibly.

Celia leaned back against the door once she

was inside her room. She closed her eyes. The throbbing in her head was easing somewhat now. A drink would probably clear it up completely. Maybe Landrum would bring a bottle with him when he slipped over here a little later.

She was sure that he would be coming to see her. They had had things to talk about before. Now, following this incident, they had even more to discuss.

There were some baffling undercurrents in this case. Could it be that someone had discovered the truth about Powell's Army? There was a great deal at stake in this mission, and if the enemy knew who she and Landrum and Glidinghawk really were, there was one very ominous possibility.

They could be heading right into a trap — a deadly one.

# CHAPTER EIGHT

The soft knock came ten minutes later. Celia had taken off her hat and coat while she was waiting, and now she went to the door and said quietly, "Who is it?"

"B and C," Landrum replied, using the operative codes for Glidinghawk and himself.

Celia let them into the room. Both men had grim expressions on their faces. As Celia shut the door behind them, Landrum went on, "What the hell was that all about?"

"I could ask you the same thing about your little performance at Madam Henrietta's tonight," Celia said coolly. "Was it just a performance, Landrum, or were you really falling down drunk?"

The Texan grinned at her. "What do you think? As long as I was there anyway, I didn't think it would do any harm to establish myself as a commission employee with a fondness for spirits.

83

Somebody might try approaching me for information, and we could get a lead that way."

Celia nodded grudging acceptance of the story. What he said made sense. She said, "So I suppose to make your pose really convincing you went upstairs with one of the girls?"

"As a matter of fact . . . I didn't. I just spent some of Amos's money buying one of them drinks. I figure as long as I'm not bedding her, the Army can pick up the tab."

"I'll be interested to see how Colonel Powell responds to your logic, Landrum," Glidinghawk put in. He turned to Celia. "Now, as our Confederate friend asked, what happened here?"

Celia rapidly filled them in on the beginning of the incident. "What I told you in the hall was true, Landrum," she said. "The man didn't steal anything. He just nosed through the whole room."

Landrum nodded thoughtfully. "It looks like somebody is suspicious of you, Celia. What happened in Madam Henrietta's office?"

The pretty young redhead felt herself blushing. "She offered me a job," Celia said.

"That's all? She didn't say anything about the commission or who's behind the effort to find out their decision?"

"Well, what did you expect her to do?" Celia asked. "Give us the answers to all our questions on a silver platter? She's a smart woman, Landrum. She's not going to giving anything away easily."

"So what do we do now?"

Celia took a deep breath. "No matter what Amos's orders said, I may have to go to work there to find any real evidence."

Landrum was shaking his head before the words were finished coming out of her mouth. "I can't let you do that, Celia. You know what you'd be expected to do. This isn't like dealing faro in a saloon back in Fort Griffin, girl."

"You want results, don't you?"

"Of course I do, but—"

Glidinghawk interrupted, "Landrum's right, Celia. It would be too unpleasant for you, not to mention downright dangerous. What did you tell the woman?"

"I told her I'd have to think about it."

Landrum nodded. "Good. That gives you an excuse to go back once more. If you don't find out anything this next time, though, we'll have to abandon this part of the plan. Gerald and I have our spots with the commission; maybe we can find out something working from that angle."

Celia felt frustration eating at her insides, but she could tell from the stern looks on the faces of Landrum and Glidinghawk that arguing with them wasn't going to do any good.

Well, if she couldn't convince them that she was right, she might have to just let them think she was going along with what they wanted—then go ahead and do what she had to do.

Glidinghawk said, "The man who was here in your room looked like the type who could be hired cheaply for a job of snooping. It's a shame he wouldn't talk about who hired him."

Celia frowned. "Where were you, by the way? You sound like you were watching the whole thing."

"Not all of it," the Omaha said. "I was down in our room when I heard the commotion in the hall. I cracked the door open and glanced out, but it looked like you and Landrum had everything under control. I thought it might be wiser not to get involved."

Celia nodded. "What do we do now?"

"Keep going," Landrum said. "Gerald and I are riding out on a geological survey tomorrow. We'll probably be out overnight, but I think we can be back the next day. You steer clear of Madam Henrietta's until we get back, understand?"

"All right," Celia sighed. "I really am old enough to take care of myself, though. After four missions, I'd think that you'd have some confidence in me."

"I've got plenty of confidence in you," Landrum replied. "But there's more than one fortune riding on this. The people involved wouldn't hesitate a second to kill you if they thought you were a threat to their plans."

Celia couldn't help but shudder at his words, because she knew they were true. On the surface, this mission might appear to be less dangerous than their others — after all, they were in the middle of a bustling city, not out in the wilderness of

Texas or Arizona or Montana—but Celia knew that the exact opposite was true.

The men they were after this time were probably the most ruthless and deadliest of all.

That thought reminded her of Roland. He had certainly looked as if he could kill without hesitation or compunction.

"Is there anything else you can tell us about what went on tonight?" Landrum asked.

"We might try to find out some more about a man named Warren Judson," Celia told him. "He was in the office with us, and from the things he and Henrietta said, he may have some connection with her business. He's her banker, I know that."

Landrum rubbed his jaw. "Banker, eh? I never have trusted those fellas. I've always felt like it was better to look after my own money than give it to some stranger. He could be tied up in this, all right. It might mean a lot to him to know where the army's going to build that new fort."

"I'll see what I can come up with while you and Gerald are gone," Celia said.

"Be subtle," Glidinghawk reminded her. "Asking too many questions can give you away."

She nodded. "I know." Maybe she could get Fox to help her, she thought. The young former second lieutenant was getting better at this. He might come in handy.

Landrum said, "I reckon we'd all better turn in. The next few days are going to be busy."

Celia lifted a hand to her aching head. "You

wouldn't happen to have a drink on you, would you, Landrum?"

He grinned at her. "After the way you acted when you thought I'd been boozing, you want me to share a nip with you?"

"My head hurts," she snapped. "I hit it against the wall when that man ran into me. I just thought a drink might get rid of my headache."

Landrum reached inside his coat and pulled out a small silver flask. "This stuff usually *causes* headaches, but since you've already got one, maybe it'll work." He uncapped it and passed it over to her. "Not too much, though."

Celia nodded and sipped the whiskey. It was raw stuff, the kind that Landrum's body was probably used to. It burned all the way down to her stomach, though, and made her blink rapidly.

"How's the head now?" Landrum asked a moment later.

Celia nodded. "Better." She handed the flask back to him, and he took a swig himself before he recapped it.

"Ahhh," he sighed. "Nothing like good corn. Puts hair on your chest." He glanced meaningfully at Celia's bosom. "Or in your case—"

"Good night, both of you," Celia said firmly.

Landrum went out with a grin, and there was even a hint of a smile on the Omaha's stoic face.


Celia spent a restless night, tossing and turning

in the hotel's bed and trying to make some sense out of everything that had happened. She had said nothing to Landrum and Glidinghawk about Major Devlin Henry's being in Madam Henrietta's office. That omission made her feel a little guilty, as if she were withholding evidence from them.

And, of course, that was exactly what she was doing. It was entirely possible that Devlin had nothing to do with their mission — but it was equally possible that he was involved with the corruption threatening the commission.

Celia was going to find out. But until she did, she was going to give Devlin the benefit of the doubt.

Because she was attracted to him? That was hardly professional behavior.

She stared up at the darkened ceiling of the hotel room and willed herself to be still. There was no way she could quiet the turmoil in her mind, however.

Dawn finally came, and somewhere in that hazy space of time, Celia slept.


"I look positively dreadful," she said aloud to her reflection the next morning. She tilted her head as she sat in front of the mirror mounted on the dresser, trying to find an angle at which the evidence of her wakeful night was less obvious.

Celia brushed her hair, the strokes short and compact and angry. Gradually, the tension she was feeling began to lessen. There was plenty for her to do today. The strands of this case might be in a jumbled mess at the moment, but if she kept working with them, sooner or later they would straighten themselves out.

By the time she went downstairs an hour later, she had made significant improvements in her appearance. Her hair was carefully combed and arranged, and she was wearing a simple but attractive green dress and a lightweight, waist-length jacket. A different clerk was on duty at the desk in the lobby, and he paid no attention to her. Evidently he had not heard about the excitement of the night before.

She had breakfast at the nearby restaurant. The sun was shining as she stepped out onto the sidewalk after the meal, but again there was a chill in the air.

The streets of Denver were busy this morning. Wagons rolled up and down the thoroughfares, raising clouds of dust on the unpaved ones. Men on horseback threaded their way among the heavy vehicles. The sidewalks were full of men and women hurrying about their business.

Celia joined the throng, moving down the street into the central business district. She was looking for banks, and she found several as she strolled along the streets. It was midmorning, however, before she found the one she was actually searching for.

In the big front window, engraved beneath the

bank's name, were the words WARREN JUDSON, PRESIDENT.

Celia nodded to herself. She had a starting point now.

She went through the double doors leading into the bank. A uniformed guard held the door for her and closed it behind her, nodding and smiling. He said, "Good morning, ma'am."

"Good morning," Celia replied. She glanced around the big room. It was high-ceilinged, and her words echoed slightly. There were several teller's cages along one wall with customers lined up in front of all but one of them. On the other side of the room were desks for the bank's employees. A door beyond the desks was closed, and a sign on it read PRIVATE. Celia had a feeling that was her objective.

She went on, "Could you tell me where I might find Mr. Judson, sir?"

"You have some business to discuss with him, ma'am?" the guard asked.

"Why, certainly. Why else would I wish to see him?"

The guard's smile became slightly embarrassed. Celia had a feeling that Judson's interest in attractive young women was well known to the people who worked for him.

"Mr. Judson's office is right over there, ma'am," the guard said, pointing to the door Celia had already noticed.

"Thank you," Celia said coolly.

She went across the bank's lobby and past the desks, well aware of the curious glances being sneaked at her by the tight-collared male employees. She paused at the door of Judson's office and knocked on it with her small, well-shaped fist.

"Who is it?" Judson's voice came from within.

Celia opened the door and put her head through. "It's Celia Burnett, Mr. Judson," she said quietly, so that her voice wouldn't carry to everyone outside. "Could I speak to you for a moment?"

Judson was sitting behind a large desk, pen poised over a ledger where he had been scribbling. A smile lit up his broad face as he put the pen down and closed the ledger. "Come in, my dear, come in." He pushed his chair back and stood up.

Celia stepped inside and closed the door behind her. "I know you must be a terribly busy man, Mr. Judson, and I appreciate your taking the time to see me."

"Never too busy to talk to a beautiful woman, Miss Burnett." His eyes played over her, lingering on the thrust of her breasts. "Please have a seat." He waved at a plush armchair in front of the desk. When Celia had settled into its overstuffed depths, he went on, "Now, what can I do for you?"

She leaned forward as best she could. "What I need, Mr. Judson, is some advice."

"Feel free, my dear," Judson said as he sat down behind the desk. He opened a humidor on the corner of the desk and took out a cigar. "Ask anything you like."

"What do you think I should do about Madam Henrietta's offer?"

Judson cocked an eyebrow as he clipped off the end of the cigar. "I should have thought that was perfectly obvious. I think you should accept, Miss Burnett. I hope fervently that you do."

Celia lowered her eyes. "I may have to. I shall be frank with you, Mr. Judson. I need money, a great deal of it. But if there was only something else I could do to earn it . . ."

"I understand," Judson said. "I can tell you're a sweet, innocent girl, Miss Burnett. But sometimes there are harsh realities in this world that we all must face."

Celia lifted her head, her gaze imploring. "Perhaps you could help me."

"Why, I already introduced you to Madam Henrietta—"

"No, I mean with a job. Perhaps here in your bank."

Judson threw back his head and laughed. Celia felt a surge of anger at this smug, arrogant man, but she forced it down. Losing her temper would not fit in with the role she was playing now.

"My dear Miss Burnett, I think it would be simply lovely to have you around here to brighten things up. A bank can be such a dreadfully solemn and boring place at times. But I'm afraid my depositors, to say nothing of the board of directors, would not allow me to place a woman in a position of such importance."

"There's nothing I can do here?"

Judson considered for a few seconds, then shook his head. "Impossible, simply impossible. It is true that I'm looking for another teller, but a woman . . . ? No, dear, it just isn't done." He paused, then went on, "I'm sorry."

Celia heaved a sigh. "Well, if there is nothing you can do . . . I appreciate everything you've done for me so far, Mr. Judson." She got to her feet.

"Just a moment," Judson said quickly. "Sit back down, please."

Celia hesitated, then sank back into the chair.

"Now, I don't want you worrying too much about all this, Miss Burnett," Judson said. "I promise you, Madam Henrietta is a fair employer and a good lady to work for. You won't find a better place anywhere. I've known her ever since she came to Denver, and we've come to be good friends. And I happen to know that if you can meet certain conditions, there is a great deal of money to be made right now."

Celia frowned. "What sort of conditions?"

Judson laughed. "Well, you're beautiful, so you've gotten a good start right there. But if you're also intelligent and able to keep a secret, that's even better."

"I can keep a secret," Celia declared. "I've always been trustworthy."

"And I can tell that you're intelligent." Judson

got around to lighting his cigar and blew out a cloud of smoke. "You tell Henrietta when you go back to see her that I think you should help her with her special customers."

"Special customers," Celia repeated.

"Henrietta will tell you all that you need to know. Now, what do you think, Miss Burnett? Have you made up your mind?"

Celia took another deep breath. "Yes, Mr. Judson, I believe I have."

"Excellent!" He got up and came around the desk to take her arm as she stood. His fingers stayed on her arm, holding her there. "I'm glad you came to see me today, Miss Burnett."

"I-I'm glad I came, too, Mr. Judson."

Without warning, his grip tightened on her arm and he pulled her toward him. Celia was not prepared, and he was too strong to resist. He dropped the cigar in a large glass ashtray on the desk and slid his other arm around her, trapping her in an embrace.

Judson's mouth came down on hers, the kiss urgent and demanding. He pressed his body against hers, crushing her against him. Celia's first impulse was to fight back, to try to escape from his grasp, but with every fiber of willpower at her command, she forced herself to relax in his arms. She made her lips pliant and responsive as his mouth ravaged hers.

When Judson finally broke the kiss, he grinned down at her and said, "You come back to Henrietta's as soon as you can, do you understand, Miss Burnett?"

"Y-Yes," Celia replied gaspingly. Her insides were roiling, but she could tell that he took her revulsion for excitement. Let him think whatever he wanted, she thought, as long as she could get out of this stuffy office soon.

Judson released her, obviously through with her for the moment. As Celia turned toward the door and tried to catch her breath, something else occurred to her and she paused. "Could I ask you one other question, Mr. Judson?"

"Of course," the banker replied.

"Who was that army officer who was in Madam Henrietta's office last night? He looked rather familiar to me."

Judson waved a hand. "Just some old friend of Henrietta's, like she said. Possibly you saw him on the train. I think he just got into town, like you."

"Oh. I wanted to be sure he wasn't connected with Madam Henrietta's business. I don't want any trouble with the army."

Judson laughed again. "Don't worry about that, my dear. The army has no intention of bothering Henrietta — and neither do any of the local authorities either. You'll be perfectly safe working there."

Celia nodded. "That's very good to know. Thank you again, Mr. Judson."

"My pleasure, Miss Burnett." And the smirk he wore said that it had indeed been a pleasure.

Again there were curious looks directed her way

as she went out through the bank's lobby. Celia knew she was probably pale from the strain of the interview with Judson. As the guard held the door for her and she stepped out onto the sidewalk, the cool air felt good. It refreshed her as she walked back toward the hotel.

On the way, she thought about what she had learned from her visit to the bank. Perhaps it had been a foolhardy thing to do — after all, Judson might have hired the man to search her room the night before — but she had at least established that Judson had an even closer connection with Henrietta LaBoeuf than they had thought. There was a good chance that Judson was one of the ringleaders in the effort to discover the commission's decision.

There was still a matter of proof, though.

That was where the other item of information she had gleaned would come in handy. Judson was looking for another teller, and he insisted that he would only hire a man for the position.

A slight smile curved Celia's lips. There had been a time, and not too long ago at that, when *man* might have been too strong a word for Preston Kirkwood Fox.

Fox had been unhappy about not having a cover identity on this mission. Now perhaps a role had been found for him. He was educated enough to handle the duties of a teller's position in a bank.

Celia knew she should discuss this with Landrum and Glidinghawk, but they were on their way out into the wilderness on their geological expedition. There was no time to waste, Celia thought. As soon as she could talk to Fox, she would outline the plan, and he could put it into effect.

With Fox working in Judson's bank, Landrum and Gerald posing as employees of the commission, and she herself in Madam Henrietta's parlor house, Powell's Army would have just about everything covered.

And all she had to do to accomplish her end of the job—

Celia shook her head and put that thought out of her mind. There would be time enough to worry about that later.

She got directions to the sheriff's office and stopped there long enough to sign the complaint against the man who had broken into her room the night before. He was still in custody and still stubbornly refusing to answer any questions about who he was or who had hired him. Celia didn't expect that situation to change anytime soon.

She had just reached the door of her hotel when a voice behind her called, "Celia!"

She stopped and turned around and, for the second time in less than twenty-four hours, was surprised to find herself face to face with Major Devlin Henry.

# CHAPTER NINE

The sun hadn't been up long that morning when Landrum and Glidinghawk rode northwest out of Denver, angling toward the mountains.

They were on horses rented from one of the local liveries and paid for by the commission. Each man also led a pack mule. One of the beasts carried their supplies, the other the equipment that would be needed for the geological survey.

Landrum had a hard time keeping his eyes open in the dawn light. There was a breeze out of the north that was downright cold at this time of day, and that helped keep him awake. Otherwise, he thought, he would have dozed off right in the saddle.

He had actually put away more liquor the night before than he had let on to either Celia or Glidinghawk. Although the drunk act at Madam Henrietta's had been just that, an act, he had had to actually swallow some of the liquor he had pretended to guzzle. And afterward, once he had nipped from the flask, it was a little hard to stop.

As they left the outskirts of town behind them, Landrum glanced over at the Omaha and muttered, "How the hell do you do it?"

"Do what?" Glidinghawk asked.

"Look so wide awake when it's still the middle of the night."

Glidinghawk grinned. "I've never let myself be corrupted by the white man's ways."

"Bullshit!" Landrum exclaimed. "What about all that time you were living with white folks in Nebraska? What about back East at that fancy Dartmouth College place?"

"I may have been surrounded by white men, but I never forgot that I was a red man." Glidinghawk's mouth quirked, and his tone became bitter as he went on, "Just as when I went back to the Omaha, I was never allowed to forget the time I had spent with the white men. Neither world wanted me."

"So you wound up with us," Landrum mused. "Reckon things sometimes work out for the best, even when we don't understand 'em."

Glidinghawk made no reply.

The Rockies loomed majestically, seemingly only a few hundred yards away, but as the two men rode through the morning, the mountains never seemed to get any closer. At one point, Landrum said, "Just what are we supposed to be doing out here anyway?"

Glidinghawk turned and reached back to the mule he was leading. He extracted a map from one of the pouches on the animal and unrolled the thick parchment.

"These maps of the area have little detail on them," he said. "You and I are supposed to fill them in with the geologic makeup of the terrain."

"And what does that mean?"

"We have to note the kinds of soil and rocks and rock formations that we see."

"What good does that do anybody?"

Glidinghawk rolled up the map again and stored it away. "It can tell a great deal to a properly trained eye. It can tell how stable the land is, how much water is available, how much erosion is going to take place under normal weather conditions. The army intends to build this fort to last, Landrum. In order to know where to put it, they have to have some idea what the territory will be like in, say, twenty or thirty years."

"And you can tell that from all this geological foofaraw?"

The Omaha grinned again. "Not I. I'm not well educated enough in that area. But I know enough to fake these maps and make it look like we know what we're doing."

"Good, because I sure as hell don't."

They rode along in silence again for a time, then Glidinghawk said abruptly, "I'm worried about Celia."

"So am I," Landrum agreed gloomily. "I don't think anybody is on to who you and I really are, but I'm not so sure about Celia. I hope she stays away from that whorehouse until we get back. I don't want her poking around there on her own."

"She has a mind of her own, that one, and a strong will to go with it. I fear she may not listen to our advice, Landrum."

"That wasn't advice," the Texan snapped. "That was orders when I told her to wait for us to get back."

"Still . . ."

Glidinghawk lapsed into silence, but the thought of Celia perhaps risking her life stayed with both men as they pushed on over the gently rolling plains.

The mountains still didn't look any closer when Landrum and Glidinghawk stopped for lunch. As they ate, Glidinghawk took out the map again and studied it. "That's Arapaho Peak," he said, pointing to one of the higher crests. "According to the markings on this map, we should be reaching the area we're supposed to study soon."

"About time," Landrum grunted. He chewed a cold biscuit and washed it down with a swallow of water from his canteen.

Glidinghawk found a pencil and a pad of paper in the supplies and began making notes as he looked around. Landrum left him to the work and concentrated on keeping an eye on their back trail.

As far as he could tell, no one was following

them. That much was encouraging.

They rode on after eating, moving more slowly now as Glidinghawk scribbled notes to himself, sketched rough topographical maps, and filled in details on the maps they had been provided. The Omaha seemed to get caught up in the work, and as they paused in the middle of the afternoon, he said, "You know, Landrum, I think I could enjoy doing something like this on a regular basis."

"For real, you mean?"

The Omaha nodded. "It's interesting work, and a man can do it without having to be around a lot of other people. I think I'd be suited for it."

Landrum stared off in the distance without replying. He knew that Glidinghawk wasn't really happy working as an undercover agent, even though he had grown fond of the other members of Powell's Army. As Glidinghawk had said earlier, he wasn't really at home in either world, the red man's or the white. The day would come, Landrum speculated, when Glidinghawk would leave, still restlessly searching for some place he could call his own.

Landrum hoped the day was a long time in coming. He liked the man, and Glidinghawk was a damned good agent.

By that evening, they had almost completed surveying the area. An hour's work in the morning would complete this part of the assignment, and then they could head back to Denver. They would probably reach town before night; at least Landrum hoped so.

Celia would be going back to Madam Henrietta's, and he wanted to be around when she did.

He just hoped she didn't disobey his orders and return to the parlor house tonight.

"Cold camp?" Glidinghawk asked as they found a likely spot and brought the animals to a halt.

Landrum shook his head. "I think a fire would be safe enough. We haven't seen a soul all day except that cowpoke chousing a couple of steers. And there's no Indian trouble around here right now."

They swung down from their saddles and began making camp. Landrum tended to the horses while Glidinghawk found enough wood for a small fire. When the blaze was going, he set the coffee pot out and took bacon and a pan from one of the saddlebags.

"Nothing like eating out under the stars," Landrum said as he settled down across the fire from Glidinghawk. He leaned back against his saddle and regarded the purpling sky. The sun was gone behind the mountains now, and the stars were indeed popping into view. The warmth of the fire felt good as the chill of night began to settle down.

The two men ate in silence for the most part. When the food Glidinghawk had prepared was gone, they settled back with cups of coffee. Landrum slipped his flask out of his coat and uncapped it one-handed with practiced ease. He hesitated as he started to pour a dollop of whiskey into his coffee cup.

Then he grunted and put the cap back on the flask. "Don't reckon I need it," he said. "Not tonight."

Glidinghawk said nothing.

He pulled the maps out again and checked through them, finally selecting one and holding the roll of parchment out to Landrum.

"What's that for?" Landrum asked.

"We'll never be using this map," Glidinghawk replied. "It would be a good idea if you made some notes and sketches on it."

Landrum frowned. "What the hell for?"

"You're supposed to be the geologist, Landrum. If anyone is watching us, how will it look if your Indian assistant does all the work?"

Landrum nodded slowly and reached for the map. "You're right. Hand me a pencil."

He spread the map on his knees and took the pencil from Glidinghawk. Frowning intently down at the map, Landrum jotted a series of numbers in one corner.

"It doesn't matter what you put on there," Glidinghawk told him. "Just so it looks like you're working on it."

Landrum nodded again. Now that the Omaha had pointed out the possibility, he could almost feel eyes watching him from the shadows. It was probably his imagination, Landrum told himself.

There probably wasn't anybody within thirty miles of them.

He sketched in a few mountains on the map, then began writing the first names of all the women he had bedded down with over the years. It took some remembering to come up with the name of the first one, and he knew he was probably forgetting some of them, but he did the best he could.

Landrum grinned as he put the names down, partially because of the good memories some of them conjured up, partially because he wondered what somebody would think if they got their hands on this map. They'd probably figure he was using some sort of code, since his work for the commission was supposed to be a secret.

He paused and handed the map back to Glidinghawk, saying, "What do you think?"

The Omaha frowned. "What's all this?"

"You said it didn't matter what I put on there. Now nod and look solemn."

Glidinghawk nodded. "I take it these are the names of your conquests."

Landrum tried not to grin too broadly. "That's right."

Glidinghawk pointed out several of them, continuing the pretense of discussing their work. "You'll have to tell me about these, Landrum. Especially this one called Kitten."

Landrum leaned back against his saddle, sighing contentedly. "Ah, Kitten. You never saw her like,

Gerald—"

A gunshot split the night.

Instinctively, Landrum hit the dirt, diving to the side and rolling away from the light of the fire. He heard the clatter of hoofbeats as he grabbed for his Colt. Across the fire, Glidinghawk was reacting the same way.

"The horses!" Landrum yelled. "They're after the horses!"

He surged to his feet. The animals had been tied to some small trees maybe twenty yards away from the camp, close by but out of the circle of light. Someone must have sneaked up and cut them loose, because Landrum could see them running now, being hazed along by a man on horseback.

Landrum jerked his gun up and triggered off a shot. He ran after the horses, Glidinghawk close behind him. Both men fired. The horse thief leaned low over the neck of his mount, riding hard now. He veered away from the other horses.

"He's giving it up," Landrum panted as he came to a stop. He fired again into the darkness, not really expecting to hit anything. Glidinghawk held his fire and slid his pistol back into his holster.

"I'd better go round up our horses," he said. "They probably won't run too far now that they're not being driven."

"I'll keep an eye open for that skunk," Landrum said. "I think he's gone, but he might come back. You reckon it was that cowhand we saw earlier?"

"Could've been," Glidinghawk said over his

shoulder as he moved off after the runaway horses. "Might have thought he could pick up some easy money by stealing our mounts."

Another sound suddenly came to Landrum's ears. More hoofbeats, but these were coming from the other direction—back toward the camp. . . .

"The camp!" Landrum yelped. "They were just drawing us off!"

Glidinghawk stopped in his tracks and spun around. In the moonlight, his face twisted in a grimace. "Come on," he grated to Landrum.

The two men ran through the night back toward the beckoning light of their campfire. As they pounded into the small clearing where they had made camp, they saw that they were too late.

"Dammit!" Landrum growled as he surveyed the looted packs. Whoever the bandits had been, they had worked quickly and messily, rummaging through the gear and dumping anything they didn't want on the ground.

Glidinghawk knelt among the debris and grunted, "Their distraction worked. They got us away from the camp by trying to steal the horses, then had a free hand to go through our things."

"What did they take?"

A smile slowly spread across the Omaha's face as he mentally cataloged their losses. "Nothing important," he announced a moment later. "And I'd say this is definitely connected with our assignment here. They took the maps we used today, Landrum. That's all."

Landrum stared for a moment, then abruptly began to laugh. "Including the one I was just working on?"

"Oh, yes," Glidinghawk answered, indulging in a chuckle himself. "I guess they hoped to glean some useful information about the commission's work. They're going to be rather disappointed, I'd imagine."

"Well, there's nothing we can do about it now. Let's go catch those horses. I don't feel like walking back to Denver in the morning."

# CHAPTER TEN

"I'm glad I found you, Celia," Devlin said as they stood in front of the hotel. "I've been wanting to talk to you since last night—"

"Please, Devlin," Celia interrupted. "I'd rather not discuss it."

A wave of acute embarrassment went through her. She had wondered what Devlin was doing at Madam Henrietta's, all right, but he could have been wondering the same thing about her. And while there might be several plausible explanations for his presence in such a place, there was only one real reason a young woman would be there.

She started to turn away from him. He reached out and caught her arm. Celia was surprised he would be so brazen as to do such a thing.

"Listen, this is important," Devlin said urgently. "I wouldn't blame you for not wanting to talk to me, not after you saw me in Madam Henrietta's.

I'd like to explain to you why I was there."

Celia wanted to hear that explanation, but if he bared his soul to her, she would feel obligated to do the same. And she didn't want to admit to him that she had gone to the parlor house to inquire about working there.

"You don't owe me any explanations, Devlin," she began.

"You're going to have one anyway," he insisted. "Tonight at dinner."

Celia shook her head. "No, really, I couldn't."

"Of course you can. And you're going to. I'll be by here at seven to pick you up. We'll go to Maxwell's. I hear it's quite an elegant place."

"Devlin, I'm sorry—"

"I won't take no for an answer, Celia." His voice was quiet and determined.

She sighed. "Very well, then. Seven o'clock." She glanced down pointedly at her arm, which he was still gripping.

Devlin released her. "I'm glad you agreed. I can be very persistent when I have to." He touched the brim of his hat. "Good day, Celia. I'll see you tonight."

As she watched him walk off down the sidewalk, she wondered what the hell this was all about.


After eating lunch, Celia went onto the sidewalk and waited until she spotted a suitable-looking small boy walking along. She put a hand out to stop him and said, "Excuse me."

The boy looked up at her in surprise and a little bit of fear. "I didn't do anything," he said quickly. "I was on my way to school right now—"

Celia shook her head and smiled, trying to put him at ease. "I don't care if you go to school or not," she told him. "I just want you to carry a message for me."

"Oh." The boy looked relieved. "I'd be glad to do that, ma'am."

Celia handed him the envelope she had prepared earlier. Inside was a note asking Fox to come to the hotel for a meeting. She gave the boy directions to the rooming house where the second lieutenant was staying, then pressed a coin into his grubby hand.

"You'll deliver the message for me?" she asked earnestly.

The boy bobbed his head. "I sure will, ma'am." He clutched the coin happily. "I'll go right now."

"Thank you."

Celia watched for a moment as he hurried off toward the boardinghouse in the next block, then she turned and went back to the hotel. No one had been paying any attention to her as she engaged the urchin's services—at least no one that she had noticed.

She was still nervous as she waited for Fox to show up.

What if he was not in his room when the boy got there? Even though Fox had been told to lay low and hold himself available, he couldn't stay in his room twenty-four hours a day.

Celia was lying down on the bed in her room, trying to force herself to relax, when the tapping came on the door.

She got up quickly and went to the door. "Who is it?"

"Preston," came the muffled answer.

Celia opened the door and let Fox slip through. As she closed it, she asked, "Did anyone see you coming here?"

He shook his head. "I don't think so, not unless that little ragamuffin was curious and followed me. But he seemed too anxious to go waste that money you gave him to do something like that."

"Good. I have a job for you, Preston." Celia opened her bag and took out some of Amos Powell's expense money. As she extended the bills to Fox, she went on, "You'll have to go buy yourself some better clothes."

"I'll very happily do that," Fox replied as he took the money. "This uniform of the common man that I've been wearing is dreadful."

Celia didn't comment on his superior attitude. That was just the way Fox was at times. Instead, she said, "I want you to see if you can get a job as a bank teller, so you'll need to dress like one. Very sedate suits, and a high collar, and so on."

Fox nodded, tucking the bills away. "I know what bank tellers look like," he said, somewhat impatiently. "Where am I going to be working?"

Celia told him how to find Warren Judson's banking establishment. "I can't guarantee that you'll get the job, but if you'll go down there today, I think there's a good chance you will. I want you to keep an eye on Judson. He seems to have some connection with Madam Henrietta." A possibility occurred to Celia. "He may even be the actual owner of the place. A respectable businessman like him would need some kind of front if he was going to own a parlor house."

Fox nodded. "I'll start right away." He glanced at her. "Do Landrum and Glidinghawk know about this?"

Celia shook her head. "They've ridden out on some sort of geological expedition for the commission. But there's no time to wait for them to get back. We have to take advantage of this opportunity right away, Preston."

"Yes. Indeed we do."

"You're sure you can handle it?"

Fox sniffed. "You seem to have forgotten who broke the Robber's Roost case. I can certainly handle an assignment like this."

Celia remembered Robber's Roost, all right. She remembered how Fox had almost gotten Landrum and Glidinghawk killed through his stubbornness, not to mention the way he had almost dumped the side of a mountain on her head. Some of the young man's plans had worked out all right, but it had been as much through sheer luck as anything.

"All right," she nodded, not wanting to argue

with Fox. "Landrum and Glidinghawk should be back in town tomorrow. Try to stay in touch with us."

Fox left the room, visibly excited about going to work. He wanted to succeed as an undercover agent, Celia had to give him that much.

The business with Fox taken care of, that left her with nothing to do for the moment.

Nothing to do but brood about her approaching dinner date with Major Devlin Henry.

Celia wondered what this night would bring.

Devlin was punctual. It was exactly seven o'clock when he knocked on her door. That punctuality was the military man in him, Celia supposed.

He was as handsome as ever in his neat uniform. He was freshly shaved, and he smelled faintly of bay rum. Holding his hat in his hand, he smiled down at her and said, "You look lovely, Celia."

She was wearing a blue silk dress that went well with her eyes and hair. "Thank you," she murmured in response to the compliment. "Would you help me with my wrap?"

"Certainly."

Devlin held the short, fur-lined jacket for her, and then she settled a pert hat that matched the dress onto her red curls. "I suppose I'm ready," she said, although she knew she was far from ready to face Devlin's questions.

"I have a carriage waiting downstairs," he said as he slipped his arm through hers. "I think you'll like Maxwell's."

Celia wasn't worried about whether or not she would like the restaurant. Her main concern was just getting through the evening.

The carriage ride reminded her of the one a couple of nights earlier when Devlin had accompanied her from the train to her hotel. Again they sat close together, and she was all too aware of the warmth and strength within him.

"What do you think of Denver so far?" he asked when they had gone a few blocks. Celia was instantly suspicious of the question, but he sounded sincere enough.

"It seems to be quite a busy city," she replied. "And the mountains are lovely, there in the distance."

Devlin nodded. "That they are. But I'm not too fond of Denver itself, or of my assignment, for that matter."

"Oh? Why's that?" She might as well pump him for some information while she still had the chance, Celia thought.

Devlin smiled rather sheepishly. "Colonel Porter, the officer in charge here, and I don't get along very well. I do my job, mind you — I'm a soldier and I know how to take orders — but it's not a very pleasant situation."

"I can't imagine your not getting along with anyone, Devlin. You're such a friendly person."

He grimaced. "You don't know Colonel Porter. Or do you?"

"No, of course not. Why would I know some army colonel?"

"You know me, don't you?" Devlin shook his head. "Don't worry about it. Colonel Matthias Porter is no concern of yours, Celia."

He made a little more small talk, and then the carriage pulled up in front of the restaurant. It was a solid-looking brick building between a mercantile store and an express office. Through its large front windows, Celia could see customers sitting at tables covered with dazzling white cloths. There were candles on each table in addition to several chandeliers suspended from the beams of the ceiling. The people seemed to be enjoying their meals very much.

Devlin hopped down lithely from the carriage and then held up his hands to assist Celia. He supported her weight as if it was nothing as she stepped down.

"Here we are," he announced. Again he slipped his arm through hers and escorted her inside. As soon as the door of the restaurant was open, a wave of delicious aromas came wafting over them, making Celia smile.

A waiter in a fancy suit met them just inside the door. "Good evening, sir," he said solemnly to Devlin.

"I sent word to hold a table for Major Devlin Henry," Devlin told him.

"Of course, sir. If you and the lady will follow me."

The warmth of the restaurant was welcome after riding in the chilly night air outside. As she and Devlin followed the waiter's gliding path among the tables, she tried to unobtrusively scan the room and see if she recognized any of the other customers. As far as she could tell, everyone here at Maxwell's was a stranger to her. Not surprising, she thought, since she had been in Denver only two days.

The waiter seated them at a small table in a corner that was considerably dimmer than the rest of the room. In addition to the tall, slender candle in the center of the table, there was also a vase holding a single flower. Where anyone had come up with a fresh flower in Denver at this time of year, Celia didn't know. But evidently Devlin Henry had made more preparations for this dinner than simply reserving a table.

As he held the chair for her while she sat, Celia again caught a whiff of bay rum. He sat down across the small table from her, a smile on his face, and said, "I'm so glad you agreed to this dinner. I've been wanting to see you again ever since we left the train."

Celia found herself wanting fervently to believe him, wanting to believe that his only interest in her was romantic. But her every instinct told her that wasn't the case. The fact that he was so blatantly ignoring their chance meeting at Madam Henrietta's only made her more suspicious.

"But we did meet again," she pointed out. "We

met at another establishment last night."

Devlin glanced at the waiter hovering nearby, and the smile on his face faltered for an instant. Then he recovered and said, "Why don't you start by bringing us some champagne, my good man?"

The waiter nodded. "Very good, sir." He moved off toward a pair of swinging doors that had to lead to the kitchen.

Lowering his voice so that he could not be overheard from the nearest table, Devlin went on, "I intended to discuss that matter with you tonight, Celia, but I thought it could wait until after we'd had dinner."

She decided to be truthful with him, at least in one respect. "I don't think I can enjoy my dinner, Devlin, so long as the subject is hanging over us like some sword."

He nodded thoughtfully. "I suppose you're right. And you do deserve an explanation. I was just so embarrassed at what you must think of me, to be in a place like that. And you're going to be even more shocked when you hear the reason I was there."

Celia frowned. He sounded as if he was the one guilty of the impropriety, not she. He certainly didn't sound angry with her because she had been at the parlor house.

Casting about for something to say, she told him, "I'm sure there's a reasonable explanation for everything, Devlin." She just wished that were true in her case.

"Oh, it's perfectly reasonable, but it doesn't reflect well on me, I'm afraid." He took a deep breath. "To put it bluntly, Celia, I was there because Henrietta used to be my wife."

Celia's breath seemed to stick in her throat. Her eyes widened, and she felt as if the floor had dropped out from under her. After a long moment, she managed to say, "Your . . . your wife?"

Devlin nodded miserably. "I told you you'd be shocked."

Celia felt a laugh starting deep inside her, and she frantically suppressed it. He was taking this so seriously. She knew his feelings would be hurt if she started to laugh. The confession had obviously taken a lot out of him.

Shocked? She had certainly never expected Devlin to reveal that he had once been married to Henrietta. She had considered practically every possibility except that. She had even wondered if they were brother and sister.

When she trusted herself to speak, she said, "You and she are no longer married?"

Devlin shook his head. "We were divorced three years ago. It was quite an ugly mess for a time. And it did nothing to help my army career, I assure you. But I've put all of that behind me now. It's a closed chapter in my life."

"Yet you were there in her house last night."

His hand clenched into a fist on the tablecloth. "It was a mistake, a foolish impulse I gave into. When I heard that she was here in Denver, I knew I should stay away from her, but curiosity got the better of me. I wanted to know how she was doing." He smiled again, this time rather bitterly. "Despite what she did to me, I still care for her in a way."

"What . . . she did to you . . . ?"

Devlin's face became bleak. "She made a fool of me — with another man. I'll say no more about it, Celia."

She reached out and put her hand on his, feeling the fist tense even tighter, then begin to relax at her touch. "We'll say no more about it," she agreed softly.

The waiter arrived with the champagne, and when they each had their glasses filled, Devlin lifted his. "To new friends," he said.

Celia clinked her glass against his. "To new friends," she agreed.

The champagne was excellent and completed the job of warming her. Devlin ordered the meal for both of them, requesting trout, potato, and salad. "It's not fancy," he said when the waiter was gone again, "but from what I've heard, the quality is very good."

"I'm sure it will be."

Celia's conscience began to gnaw at her, as she had worried that it would. Devlin had been honest with her — she was sure that he was telling the truth about Henrietta — and she had still not offered him any kind of explanation about her presence at the parlor house.

"Devlin," she said quietly, "you haven't asked me what I was doing there last night."

He gave a curt shake of his head. "That's none of my business, Celia."

"You have as much right to know about me as I have to know about you."

"No, Celia, I wanted to tell you about Henrietta, because I knew that you wouldn't . . . wouldn't pass judgment on me. You're not that kind."

"And neither are you," she insisted. She pressed on, "I was there for one reason and one reason alone, Devlin. I was inquiring about the possibility of obtaining employment there."

She felt herself blushing hotly as she said it. A part of her brain told her wryly that she was taking her cover identity too seriously. She was hardly an innocent virgin, after all. That state of affairs had been permanently altered during the first mission of Powell's Army.

Devlin looked down at the table, ever the perfect gentleman. "I have no right to make any comment on that, Celia," he told her. "I like you a great deal, but I have no claim on you—yet."

Celia's heart gave a tiny leap at the implication in his words. She wanted to impulsively lean across the table and give him a kiss, but he was an officer and a gentleman. Such brazen behavior would probably just shock him.

"There is something else I have to tell you, Devlin," she said, steeling herself to go on. "I'll be going back to Madam Henrietta's."

He nodded. "Whatever you wish."

"Because she offered me a job, and I have to go back to tell her I refuse."

A smile slowly stretched across Devlin's face. "You're not going to work for her?"

Celia shook her head and said, "I just decided tonight. I can't accept the offer."

Her hand was still resting on his. Now his fingers twined with hers and tightened. "I'm glad to hear it," he said. "It's not very gallant to say it, but Henrietta is not a good person, Celia. She's certainly not the person I thought I had married."

"I understand."

Celia felt the lightness of relief now that the air was clear between them. Each of them had been truthful, although Celia had certainly omitted several important portions of her story—such as being an undercover operative for the U.S. Army.

But she was sure now that Devlin had no connection with the assignment that had brought her here. From this point forward, any relationship between them could develop naturally and take whatever course it would, without everything being distorted by lies and deception.

And the burden of considering Madam Henrietta's offer had been lifted from her, too. Landrum had insisted all along that Celia follow Powell's orders and not go to work in the parlor house, but to be honest, she had been leaning in the direction of disobeying. That had seemed like the best way to get the information they needed.

But as Landrum had said, he and Glidinghawk had their posts within the commission, and now Preston Fox might also be on the inside—if Judson was involved in the case and if Fox had gotten the job in the bank. Celia wished she had had the chance to talk to Fox again before coming out to dinner. She wondered if he had been successful in his assignment.

The one overriding factor in her decision, however, was sitting across the table from her, smiling into her eyes.

She was falling in love with Devlin Henry. There was no way she could work for Madam Henrietta now.

The realization started a quiver of emotion deep within her. She was in love, really in love for maybe the first time in her life. There had been a man in Fort Griffin, of course, and she would never forget the gambler called Black Jack, but what she was feeling now for Devlin Henry was different. It was stronger, deeper.

Tomorrow night, she decided, she would go back to Madam Henrietta's and tell the woman what to do with her offer of employment. After that—after this case was over—Celia would have another decision to make.

Could Powell's Army get along without her?

Would Devlin want her as his wife?

Questions, so many questions. Celia's head was swimming with them—or maybe it was the champagne. Whatever, she was feeling as happy and giddy as she could ever remember feeling.

"You've gotten awfully quiet," Devlin said. "What are you thinking?"

Celia smiled. "Good thoughts," she said. "Only good thoughts."

# CHAPTER ELEVEN

"Good day, madam," Preston Kirkwood Fox said to the prune-faced old woman who had just deposited two whole dollars in her account. The woman moved away from the window, and her place was taken by a burly man who smelled strongly of horse manure.

Fox sighed and tried to keep a polite expression on his face. When working with the public, one had to have thick skin and a strong stomach. Still, Fox yearned for the days when he had been surrounded by military discipline. If the citizens of Denver had been under his command, he would have whipped them into shape soon enough.

"How can I help you, sir?" Fox asked the customer.

The man thumped a filthy canvas bag onto the counter of Fox's window. The jingle of coins came from within the bag.

"Had these buried in my stable," the man grunted. "Got to thinkin' I better come put 'em in the bank before somethin' happened to 'em."

Fox swallowed. "Do you have an account here, sir?"

"Not yet. Reckon I'd better start one, eh?"

"I suppose. Do you know how much is in this, ah, container of yours?"

The man shook his head. "Got no idea. You can count 'em, though, can't you?"

Fox closed his eyes for a moment. He considered how effective a few public floggings might be in bringing the public into line. Then he sighed again and said, "Of course. I'll count them."

The bank was busy this morning. There were four people in line at Fox's window behind the odorous stableman, and the other tellers were occupied with customers as well. Warren Judson's establishment seemed to be quite successful.

Fox wasn't sure why Celia suspected the man. Judson already seemed like a rather admirable individual to him, even though Fox had only met him the previous afternoon. The banker ran his business efficiently, with an eye toward maximum profits. If there was one thing that Fox admired, it was efficiency.

However, Fox remembered all too well his misjudgments of other people in the past. His ability to read character had never been his greatest asset, and he was reluctantly coming to realize that.

This was his first morning on the job. He had

come to the bank yesterday afternoon following his talk with Celia. Attired in a newly purchased suit, he had obviously impressed Judson with his manners and intelligence as he inquired about the availability of the teller's position. Judson had hired him on the spot after Fox had invented a phony history of having been employed at some of the largest banks in New York and Philadelphia.

So far, the work itself had been easy. To someone who had been at West Point, the task of adding and subtracting money was simple. Fox was confident he would be able to handle any chore that Judson gave him.

Finding evidence that Judson was involved in the effort to discover the commission's decision would be more difficult.

Fox was never alone in the bank. If he had been, he would have tried to get into Judson's private office and go through his records. Perhaps if he worked himself into a position of trust —

"What the hell you doin', boy? You're supposed to be countin' that money!"

Fox shook his head, his reverie shattered. He looked down and found that he had no idea where he had been in his count of the stableman's coins. He would have to start over on the smelly job.

"Sorry," he muttered as he began counting again.

Despite the unpleasantness of having to deal with the public, the morning went quickly. Fox noticed that Judson came out of his office several times and looked around, as if he was checking to make sure that everything was running smoothly in the lobby. Once, Judson caught his eye and nodded, and Fox knew the banker was reassuring him that he was doing fine. Fox smiled, pleased to be in a position of trust and responsibility.

At noon, the head teller signaled to Fox to close his window. Fox completed the transaction in which he was engaged, then gratefully slid down the shutter which closed off his window just as a young, harried-looking woman with two small children in tow stepped up. At least he wouldn't have to deal with them.

The head teller stepped around the partition between his cage and Fox's. "You've got half an hour for lunch," he said. "I'd advise you not to take any longer. Mr. Judson is quite strict about that."

Fox nodded. "Thanks. Is there a good place to eat around here?"

The dour-faced head teller lifted a small sack in his hand. "You should do like I do. My wife prepares my lunch. Saves time and money."

"I'm afraid I don't have a wife," Fox smiled.

"That's not my problem. But marriage teaches a man efficiency. You'd do well to remember that, Fox."

Fox nodded solemnly. Being an undercover agent was no job for a married man, but he couldn't very well tell his coworker that.

He left the bank through the rear door, which

had to be unlocked for him by a guard stationed there. There was a small peephole cut into the door so that when employees returned, the guard could check their identity before admitting them.

Fox found a small, inexpensive dining counter in the next block. The food was not very good, but it was near the bank and he had no trouble getting back to work on time.

Early in the afternoon, his feet began to hurt. The shoes he had purchased were smart and highly polished, but he had to admit that they had perhaps not been a wise choice for long hours of standing. There was nothing he could do about it now, though, except suffer through the rest of the afternoon.

As the twinges of pain came more and more frequently and began to spread into his calves, Fox became more curt with the customers. Several left his window frowning. He knew he should be making an effort to control his irritation. If the customers complained to Judson and he lost his job as a result, then all of this would have been for nothing.

Still, it was hard to be pleasant when imps were plunging knives into his toes every time he shifted his weight.

There was a large clock on the wall of the lobby. Fox could see it from his post, and the hands seemed to take forever to crawl around its face. The bank closed at three o'clock. Surely he could make it that long.

And then he could get off his feet. Blessed relief! He was counting the seconds until that time.

At fifteen minutes until three, several men wearing boots and jeans and long dusters came through the bank's double doors. In this case the garments were well named, because the coats were covered with trail dust. The men had the broad brims of their hats pulled low over their faces. As they started across the lobby toward Fox's window, the guard at the door stared after them suspiciously.

Fox had just finished dealing with a recalcitrant old-timer who refused to see that he had made a mistake in adding up his deposit. He had finally gotten that straightened out and was looking forward to a short breather, because the old man had been the last customer in his line at the moment. But then Fox looked up and saw the cowboys ambling toward him, and he sighed wearily. No doubt they were ranch hands come to deposit whatever pittance was left over from their most recent forty-a-month-and-found.

Two of the men came to the window. The other two spread out, one going to each side. Fox frowned, wondering what they were doing. As the two men stepped up to the window, he asked, "What can I do for you gentlemen?"

Both men yanked heavy guns from their holsters. "You can give us all the money you got back there, you goddamn pansy!" one of them growled. He pressed the muzzle of his pistol against Fox's nose for emphasis.

Fox gasped. They had moved so fast that he had had no time to react. Tucked behind his belt in the small of his back was a small Smith & Wesson revolver, less than half the size of the big Colt that was painfully gouging his nostrils. If he reached for it, though, he knew damned well that his brains would be splattered all over the cage.

Fear spasmed through him as he crossed his eyes and stared down at the barrel of the gun. It was all he could do to control his bodily functions and keep from fouling himself. He heard a woman scream and a man curse as the bank's customers realized that a robbery was taking place, but the sounds seemed to come from far away.

Without taking his eyes off the gun, Fox felt for the handle of his cash drawer. He found it and yanked the drawer out. The second outlaw reached through the window and over the counter with his free hand and started grabbing up all the bills he could touch. He cackled and said, "Fancy little sumbitch is too scared to move, Lew. Whyn't you just shoot him and get him out of the way?"

Fox's eyes widened more at the words. A part of his brain was demanding urgently that he do something. He couldn't just stand here and let these desperadoes rob the bank —

But there was nothing he or anyone else could do. One of the other bandits had the guard and the customers covered, while the fourth man was menacing the other employees with a sawed-off shotgun he had pulled from under his duster. A weapon like that could shred a man into so much raw meat at close range.

"Hurry up, Joe," the robber holding the gun on Fox snapped to his companion. "We've still got those other cages to clean out."

Joe laughed again as he stuffed money inside his coat. "I'm gettin' it, I'm gettin' it," he said.

Fox kept his hands in plain sight, the fingers trembling. There was a chance he would make it out of this alive if he just stayed still and didn't threaten the outlaws. Suddenly, out of the corner of his eye, he saw movement —

Warren Judson opened the door of his office and stepped out, stopping in his tracks and staring in shock when he saw what was happening. "My God!" he exclaimed, then lifted his voice in a furious howl. "Help! It's a holdup! Help!"

"Tarnation!" the bandit called Lew yelped. He jerked the gun away from Fox's face and started to turn it toward the yelling Judson. Fox knew he intended to shoot the banker down.

The sack of coins that had been brought in earlier by the stableman was still on the shelf underneath Fox's counter. He should have put them away by now, he knew, but he had been avoiding handling them as much as possible.

Now, without really thinking about it, he scooped up the bag and threw it between the bars of his window as hard as he could.

The heavy bag hit the outlaw's hand just as he

pulled the trigger. The gun blasted, but Lew's aim had been knocked off. The slug shattered one of the big windows in the front of the bank and whined off outside.

Fox suddenly discovered that terror could increase a man's efficiency just as much as marriage. He swept the tails of his coat aside with his left hand and jerked the Smith & Wesson out with his right. The outlaw called Joe started to yell a warning when Fox triggered his first shot.

At this range, the little revolver packed plenty of punch. The bullet caught Joe in the chest. He rocked back a step, dropping his gun, then folded up in the middle and collapsed on the floor, a look of surprise frozen in his now-dead eyes.

Lew spun toward Fox, shooting curses. Fox spasmodically squeezed the trigger twice more. The first slug burned across the outlaw's cheek, leaving a raw red streak. The second hit him just under the nose, boring into the base of his brain and dropping him lifeless to the floor, where he twitched for several seconds before becoming forever still.

Seizing the opportunity of the distraction, the guard at the door went for his gun. He got it out and fired once at the man who had been covering him. The bullet hit the man in the thigh, spinning him around. The bandit's pant leg turned crimson as blood from a severed artery soaked the cloth. He shrieked in pain, a high, thin, nerve-grating sound.

The bandit with the shotgun jerked the muzzles of his ugly weapon toward the guard and blasted one barrel at him. The buckshot slammed the guard against the wall. He bounced off and pitched forward on his face, his gun skittering away out of nerveless fingers.

Before the shotgunner could fire again, Warren Judson had lunged across the room, locking his fists together into a club. Judson was a big man, and he hit the rather small outlaw from behind with all of his weight, slamming his fists into the back of the man's neck. There was a sharp pop as bone snapped.

The shotgun thumped to the floor, followed an instant later by the bandit's body.

It was over. Fox leaned on the counter of his cage, gun in hand, drawing in great lungfuls of air. His pulse was racing, the blood pounding like a drum in his head.

Judson came over to Fox's window as the customers, freed of the menace, stampeded out of the bank and into the street. No sooner were they clear of the door than several deputies, guns drawn, bounded into the bank.

"You're too late," Judson grunted at them. He waved at the bodies sprawled around the bank's lobby. "You can haul this garbage out of here, though. One of them's still alive, I believe."

The leg-shot bandit was alive, although he had passed out and gone into shock from loss of blood. Fox didn't think he would live out the next hour.

One of the deputies turned over the guard's body and grimaced at the damage done by the shotgun. "Alvin never had a chance," he said.

"He was doing his job," Judson replied. He glanced through the bars of the window at Fox. "Just as this gallant young man was. Come out of there, Fox."

Fox was a little surprised to find that his legs worked. He walked shakily out the back of the cage and around to the door that led into the lobby. Judson met him and slapped him on the back heartily.

"Excellent work, young man," Judson congratulated him. "You certainly saved the bank a great deal of money today, not to mention putting an end to two careers of banditry. There'll be a little extra for you in your first pay envelope, I assure you."

"Th-thank you, Mr. Judson," Fox managed to say. He made his voice firmer and went on, "Like you said, I was just doing my job and protecting the bank's money."

"I won't forget this, son," Judson promised him. "I have a feeling you're going to go a long way in this business, Fox, perhaps faster than you envisioned." Judson lowered an eyelid in an exaggerated wink. "I pay my debts, boy. You'll see."

"Thank you, sir."

Fox's mind was whirling. Through pure luck, he had gotten closer to his objective on his first day at the bank. Judson was in his debt now, and Fox intended to use that to his advantage. Landrum wouldn't be able to complain about this development.

If only he hadn't had to risk being shot to accomplish it, Fox thought.

And on top of everything else, his feet still hurt.

# CHAPTER TWELVE

The sun was dipping toward the crests of the Rockies when Landrum and Glidinghawk rode back into Denver. Both men were tired, and that weariness showed in the way they slumped in their saddles.

They had encountered no more trouble during the day. Although their maps had been stolen, Glidinghawk had improvised, making crude sketches of the terrain and filling them in from memory as best he could. They were far from outstanding examples of the science of cartography, but they were best the Omaha could do.

Actually, catching the horses the night before had been the hardest task they had faced. The rented animals had been thoroughly spooked, and Landrum and Glidinghawk had been forced to chase them for the better part of an hour before they had all four of the horses rounded up.

"Are we going to the Colorado House to report in?" Glidinghawk asked as they rode past the territorial capitol.

Landrum shook his head. "That can wait until morning. You know, I've been thinking, Gerald."

"What about?"

"Just who knew where we were going, partner?"

Glidinghawk shrugged. "Colonel Porter and Tom Rainsford knew, certainly. Any number of other people could have found out easily enough. Do you suspect that either Porter or Rainsford sent those men to raid our camp?"

"It seems likely to me," Landrum nodded. "It wouldn't be the first time somebody's sold out the army."

"But why have our maps stolen?" Glidinghawk asked. "We would have been turning them in to the commission in a couple of days anyway."

"We'd have been turning them over to the whole commission," Landrum pointed out. "Maybe somebody wanted to get a jump on the other commissioners."

Glidinghawk nodded thoughtfully. "Could be, I suppose. Or maybe they just wanted to delay things for a while."

"That's a possibility, too."

It was still a tangled mess as far as Landrum could see, and he mentally cursed Amos Powell for saddling them with this assignment. Give him a gang of owlhoots to chase or a band of ornery redskins to trade shots with any day, Landrum thought.

He was still worried about Celia, too, and he was anxious to get back to the Royal Hotel and make sure she was all right. She had a redhead's temper and impulsiveness at times. Those weren't very good traits for an undercover agent, at least not most of the time.

But there was one overriding need that Landrum felt, and he knew he was going to have to take care of it before he did anything else.

"I don't suppose you want a drink, do you?" he asked Glidinghawk.

The Indian laughed shortly and shook his head. "I do not care for saloons, Landrum, you know that. But you go ahead. I'll return the horses to the livery and take our gear back to the hotel."

Landrum eyed the saloon they were passing. The light from inside was warm and beckoning in this autumn dusk, and even though the doors were closed, he could hear the strains of tinny music coming from a player piano.

He swung down out of the saddle and passed the reins to Glidinghawk. "Thanks, Gerald. I won't be long. We'll go see Celia as soon as I get there."

Glidinghawk nodded and heeled his mount into motion again, leading Landrum's horse and the two pack horses. Landrum turned toward the saloon and wiped the back of his hand across his mouth. He still had a little whiskey in the little flask he carried, but solitary swigging wasn't as satisfying as a drink in a good saloon.

In this kind of weather, the batwings were fastened back on each side of the entrance, and the doors themselves were closed. Landrum grasped the knob of one and turned it, pushing it open and stepping through into hot, smoky air. The clink of glasses, the click of poker chips, and the laughter of women who were no better than they had to be washed over him.

*Home ...*

The saloon was doing a brisk business. Most of the tables were occupied, and there were quite a few men at the bar. Landrum made his way through the crowd and found an open spot at the bar. He leaned an elbow on the hardwood and propped his foot on the brass rail next to the floor. When one of the bartenders looked the inevitable question at him, Landrum said, "Whiskey. And a beer to wash it down with."

As the unsmiling bartender set the shot of liquor and the mug of beer in front of Landrum, the Texan suddenly caught a snatch of conversation from farther down the bar. "—shot two of them himself, he did. Leastways, that's what I heard. Reckon any more of them outlaws will think twice before they try to rob old man Judson's bank again."

Landrum frowned. He tossed off the whiskey and then turned toward the speaker. Judson's name had caught his attention, and now he wanted to hear more.

The man talking was a townie, and he was going on to a friend of his about the daring actions of someone who worked in Judson's bank. For what Landrum could make out as he sipped his beer, four cowboys had tried to hold the place up, and one of the tellers had foiled them by his quick, deadly action.

The second man was nodding as the first one spun the yarn, and when the speaker paused for breath in his colorful recital, the other said, "Yep, I reckon that feller Fox is quite a hero, all right."

Landrum stiffened. Fox? Not Preston Kirkwood Fox? Surely not.

But he didn't wait to hear more. He polished off his beer, thumped the mug back onto the bar, and spun a coin to the waiting bartender. Then Landrum was on his way out, pushing between several men in his hurry to get to the door. He ignored the angry calls behind him and stalked out into the gloom.

The hotel was only a couple of blocks away from the saloon. Landrum walked it in a hurry. Darkness was settling down now, and it matched his mood. The relief he had felt at being back in Denver and having a drink had faded away. It had been replaced by a hunch that a lot had happened while he was gone.

Fox a hero? Fox gunning down two desperate outlaws? Well, stranger things had happened, Landrum supposed, although for the life of him he couldn't remember what.

He went quickly through the hotel lobby, giving the clerk a nod in reply to the man's greeting. "That Indian of yours just went up," the clerk called after him.

Glidinghawk was in their room. He saw the intense look on Landrum's face as soon as the Texan opened the door. "What's wrong?" Glidinghawk asked.

"Don't know," Landrum said. "Let's go see Celia."

They went down the hall toward her room, both men moving quietly out of habit. Landrum knocked on her door, and a moment later came the soft question, "Who's there?"

"Me and Glidinghawk," he answered. He glanced up and down the hall. "Open up. It's clear. There's nobody around."

He could see the excitement on Celia's face as she opened the door to let them in. There was something else there, too. Something that—if Landrum hadn't known better—he would have sworn was love.

Fox was standing inside the room. He looked worked up about something, too, although Landrum could tell it wasn't romance. As Celia shut the door, Landrum said to Fox, "What are you doing here?"

"Haven't you heard?" Fox asked smugly. "I'm a hero."

Landrum had been afraid he was going to say that.

The puzzled looks on the faces of Landrum and Glidinghawk gradually went away as Celia explained what she had been doing since they left. It had been an eventful two days.

Celia omitted part of the story, however. She didn't go into detail about her dinner with Devlin Henry or the choice that was facing her. She did tell Landrum and Glidinghawk about her decision not to accept Madam Henrietta's offer of employment.

"Glad to see you're making sense," Landrum grunted. "I don't know what possessed Amos to send you in there in the first place."

Celia didn't reply. Actually, she was thinking, it would have been a good idea if she had worked at the parlor house. She would have been in the best position of all of them to obtain the information they needed.

Now, of course, that was out of the question. With the way she and Devlin felt about each other, there was no way she could submit to the degradation of an inmate's life, even in the line of duty.

"I'm going to Madam Henrietta's tonight to tell her my decision," Celia went on.

Landrum nodded. "I reckon I can be there, too. Gerald and I have been pretty busy, but I reckon I can manage a night at Madam Henrietta's." Quickly, he told Celia and Fox about the raid on the camp and the stolen maps.

"But you're tired, Landrum," Celia protested when he was finished. "Besides, they'll probably remember you from the other night. They won't even let you in after the drunken scene you made."

"She has a point, Landrum," Fox put in. "Besides, I'm going to be there myself. I can keep an eye on Celia."

Celia turned toward him. "You hadn't told me that."

"I hadn't gotten around to it. Warren Judson invited me to accompany him to the house tonight. I'm to consider it partial repayment for the favor I did him this afternoon."

"I did hear something about that," Landrum said.

Glidinghawk spoke up. "Well, I haven't. What the hell happened?"

Quickly, with as many flourishes as he could work in, Fox told them about the attempted holdup at Judson's bank. He told the truth about his own actions but left out any mention of the paralyzing fear he had felt during most of the robbery. When Fox finished his recitation, Landrum grunted and said, "You'd better be careful, Preston. You'll get a reputation as a fast gun if you keep this up."

"And what's wrong with that?" Fox demanded.

"You'll have every two-bit punk and would-be gunslinger in the territory looking you up," Glidinghawk told him. "They'll all want to be known as the man who shot down Preston Fox."

Fox paled, and his Adam's apple bobbed up and down as he swallowed nervously. Clearly, he had not thought of this possibility. He said. "It . . . it wasn't like a regular gunfight or anything—"

"That won't matter," Landrum said. "What's important is that you've got a couple of notches on your gun now. I'd watch my back, was I you."

Although there was some truth in what Landrum and Glidinghawk said, most of it was just ribbing on their part, trying to take the self-satisfied Fox down a notch. Celia could tell that, even though Fox couldn't. And they seemed to have succeeded, to judge from the trepidation visible on Fox's narrow features.

"When are you supposed to get together with Judson, Preston?" Celia asked him to get his mind off the subject.

"Ah . . . at eight o'clock." Fox pulled out his pocket watch and checked the time. "I should be moving along, I suppose. Mr. Judson told me to meet him at Madam Henrietta's. I don't want to be late."

Landrum made a ribald comment about remembering that once he got inside the house. His face red, Fox slipped out of the room.

"I'd better be going soon myself," Celia said. "I don't want to put this off any longer." She put a hand on Landrum's arm. "Why don't you and Gerald go get some rest?"

"I don't know," the Texan said dubiously. "I'm not sure about relying on Fox to protect you if anything happens."

"Nothing's going to happen, Landrum." Celia's voice was confident.

He gave a reluctant nod. "You come right back here when you're through, hear?"

"I will," Celia promised.

Actually, she was supposed to meet Devlin here for a late supper. Nothing was going to delay her and keep her from that.

Celia checked the hall. A drummer was going into one of the rooms down the corridor. As soon as his door was closed behind him, she motioned for Landrum and Glidinghawk to slip out. They started back to their room.

Celia felt the emotions building within her as she got ready to go out. This was going to be an important night. It marked the end of her phase of this assignment.

And the beginning of something much bigger, she hoped.

# CHAPTER THIRTEEN

Preston Fox felt an undeniable surge of excitement as he descended from the carriage in front of Madam Henrietta's. At the same time, he was nervous. He knew what kind of place this was, and despite what had happened at Robber's Roost, he was still pretty inexperienced with women.

He couldn't help but wonder what kind of companion he would wind up with this evening and how he would handle the situation. There was also the worry that he might run into one of the officers from the commission who could recognize him from the days when he was still in uniform.

But in spite of those anxieties, Fox was looking forward to this.

He was wearing a more elegant suit than the one he had purchased for his work in the bank. He had bought it this afternoon, after Judson had issued the invitation to join him here tonight, and while Fox wasn't sure how Amos Powell would feel about the expenditure, in Fox's mind it was perfectly justified.

After all, he was on the verge of moving into Judson's inner circle. If the banker liked him and trusted him, there was a greater likelihood that Fox would discover something valuable.

An expensive Homburg was perched on his slicked-down hair, and he carried a silver-headed walking cane. These items had been paid for with his own carefully hoarded funds—Powell couldn't complain about them.

The door opened as he approached. The burly man who stood there to welcome him smiled. "You'd be Mr. Fox," he said. "Mr. Judson told me to expect you and gave me your description."

"That's right, my good man," Fox replied casually. He expected people to recognize a man of his stature, abruptly acquired though that celebrity was. "I take it Mr. Judson has already arrived."

"Yes, sir. Come right in. He's at his private table."

Fox followed the man through the foyer and into the parlor. There was a buzz of conversation as he entered, and he imagined that it was all about him. At least that was what he wanted to believe.

His guide led him through the parlor and into the dining room. As he left the parlor, Fox felt several pairs of eyes watching him and glanced over his shoulder to smile at the beautiful, daringly clad girls who were following his progress. They were a far cry from the whores who had frequented Madam Varnish's place at Robber's Roost, just as this house was infinitely more elegant and stylish than that frontier saloon and brothel.

Still, Fox felt a momentary tug at his heart as he remembered Ching Ping. The Chinese girl had been every bit as beautiful as any of these women; to him, in fact, she had been far lovelier.

But she was gone now, forever out of his reach, living a new life. He had to content himself with the knowledge that he had helped her out of a horrible predicament.

And for a time, he had loved her. . . .

"Well, hello, Preston!" Warren Judson's voice boomed in greeting. The banker stood up from a large table that was somewhat isolated from the others in the room by a partition and several good-sized potted plants. Judson went on, "So glad you could make it to my little celebration. Not every night a man has as much to celebrate as I have tonight."

Fox shook the hamlike fist that Judson extended to him. "Thank you for inviting me," he said.

"Wouldn't be having a party without you, my boy. In fact, I'd probably be mourning the loss of more money than I can afford! But you did for those robbers, son, and I'm proud of you."

Fox felt a passing twinge in his belly as he remembered how that gun barrel had been jammed against his nose. He swallowed and smiled and said, "Thank you, sir."

"Sit down, sit down!" Judson bellowed. He waved at the other people at the table. "I'll introduce you to all these folks."

As Fox sat down, he glanced around at the table's other occupants. There were four of them, three women and a man. Fox paid little attention to the man, a thin, almost colorless individual wearing spectacles. The women were the ones who drew his gaze.

Sitting at the other end of the table from Judson was a beautiful brunette, the oldest of the three females. She was only around thirty, however, and her maturity only added to her loveliness.

"Son, meet Madam Henrietta LaBoeuf," Judson said. "She runs this place, and you won't find a sharper businesswoman in the country."

"I'm so pleased to meet you, Mr. Fox," Madam Henrietta purred with a smile. "I've heard so much about you."

"And it's an honor to meet you, ma'am," Fox replied. He didn't mention that he had also heard a great deal about her—some of it in the dispatch from Colonel Amos Powell.

"That fellow beside her is Roland, Madam Henrietta's right-hand man," Judson continued.

Fox nodded to the man, who seemed unim-

152

pressed to be meeting the hero of the bank holdup.

"And now for these two lovelies," Judson said gustily. He had a girl on each side of him, and he reached out with both hands to caress their bare, creamy shoulders. As he patted the blonde to his right, the one seated next to Fox, he said, "This is Melinda, Preston. I've chosen her especially for you. And this raven-haired beauty over here is Jasmine. She's mine, at least for the night!" The banker laughed boisterously.

Fox felt a flush of embarrassment at the man's bluntness. Even though he was well aware of what purpose these girls would serve, there was no need to bellow it out like that.

He turned to Melinda and said, "I'm pleased to meet you."

Her voice was low and throaty as she replied, "And I'm very pleased to meet you, Mr. Fox."

Her hair was long and golden, and as Fox stared into her eyes, he thought that they were the deepest, richest blue he had ever seen.

He felt a pang of pure desire go through him.

The girl called Jasmine was equally beautiful. Her thick, wavy hair was as midnight black as the bird to which Judson had compared it, and there was an exotic cast to her features which spoke of some mixed blood in her veins. She regarded Fox with sleepy-lidded eyes.

"Here now, Jasmine," Judson said to her. "Don't go staring at the boy like that. You're with me, remember?"

She turned her attention back to the banker. "Of course, Mr. Judson. It's just that Mr. Fox is such a handsome young man."

Judson frowned, and Fox felt uncomfortable. Melinda was leaning closer to him now, and he suddenly felt the feather-light touch of her hand on his leg. She ran her fingers over the fabric of his pants. The fingertips seemed to leave white-hot trails that burned through the material.

"Jasmine is such a flirt," Melinda said softly. "But she's right about one thing—you are handsome, Preston. You don't mind if I call you Preston, do you?"

Fox swallowed. "N-no. Not at all."

As much as he was enjoying the sensation of Melinda rubbing her hand over his inner thigh underneath the table, he wished she would stop. There was a time and a place for such things, and this was neither.

Evidently Madam Henrietta felt the same way. She said in a quiet but firm voice, "There's no need to get carried away, ladies. We're here to have dinner, remember?"

Melinda pouted slightly. Jasmine gave the blond girl a haughty look. Fox admittedly had little experience with this sort of thing, but he felt that there was some sort of long-standing friction between the two girls.

A pair of red-jacketed waiters appeared, bearing silver trays full of food. No one had asked Fox what he wanted, so he assumed that the choice was out of his hands. As the meal was spread out on the table, he certainly had no complaints. The roast beef looked to be tender and succulent, the vegetables crisp and fresh. All in all, he discovered as he dug in with the others, an outstanding meal.

His glass was kept filled with champagne, and the liquor was almost as dizzying as the conversation between Judson and Madame Henrietta. Fox tried briefly to join in the repartee, but he knew immediately that he was out of his depth. The banker and the madam were obviously old, intimate acquaintances. It was highly possible, Fox thought, that Judson owned this place, or at least a share of it.

The time went quickly. Fox had trouble remembering that he was here in the line of duty—this part of the assignment, at least, had been highly enjoyable. Melinda was quiet for the most part, but Fox could smell the heady scent she wore, and the shy, seductive smiles she gave him completed the assault on his senses.

When the meal was over, the waiters reappeared with after-dinner brandies. Judson lit a cigar and leaned back expansively in his chair. He reached out and idly caressed Jasmine.

"My compliments, Henrietta," the banker said. "As always, you know how to treat a man."

"Thank you, Warren," Madam Henrietta smiled. She stood up. "Now, as much as I have enjoyed this evening, I do have a business to tend to."

As Henrietta got to her feet, Fox scraped his chair back and also stood, the habit too strong to break in him. Henrietta smiled at him.

"You're a gentleman as well as a daring thwarter of bank robbers, Mr. Fox," she said. Glancing at Judson and Roland, she went on, "Perhaps some others around here could learn some manners from you."

Judson barked a curt laugh. "You and I have known each other too long for such courtesies, my dear. We're like an old married couple."

Madam Henrietta's smile held daggers. "Not completely, Warren, darling." She looked at her assistant. "Come along, Roland."

Roland got to his feet and followed her without a word. That left Fox and Judson alone at the table with Melinda and Jasmine.

"Well, ladies," Judson said, grinning around the cigar in his mouth, "shall we adjourn upstairs?"

"Whatever you want," Jasmine replied sweetly.

Melinda leaned against Fox's arm. He could feel the soft thrust of her breast pressing into his side. "Are you ready, Preston?" she asked.

Fox smiled nervously. "Of course," he said. "Whenever you are."

Arm in arm, the two couples went into the parlor and then started up the broad curving staircase to the second floor. Fox was well aware that many eyes were on him, and he tried to look nonchalant as he squired the beautiful Melinda.

He wondered where Celia was and if she had had her meeting with Madam Henrietta yet. Fox knew he was supposed to have come tonight to keep an eye on her, but there didn't seem to be anything he could do about the things that had interfered with his plan.

After all, this little celebration was Warren Judson's idea, and Fox had to stay on the banker's good side.

Yes, indeed, Preston Fox told himself. Anything that went on tonight was strictly in the line of duty.

Celia was nervous when she arrived at Madam Henrietta's. She wasn't sure how the older woman would react when she heard the decision Celia had made. At the same time, there was an undeniable excitement and anticipation within the attractive young redhead.

Tonight was one more step in her relationship with Devlin Henry.

The doormen recognized her from two nights earlier and had leering grins of welcome for her. Evidently they thought she was going to be working there and that they might get to enjoy her company at some time.

If that was the case, they were going to be sorely disappointed, Celia thought. But she smiled at them anyway and said, "I've come to see Madam Henrietta."

"Figured you'd be back," one of the men said. "And so did Madam Henrietta. She's been looking forward to seeing you."

"Should I go on up to her office?"

The other man shook his head and tugged on a silken bell pull. "Just wait here a minute," he said.

Celia speculated that the bell pull rang a signal in Madam Henrietta's office. Sure enough, a few moments later the man called Roland appeared in the foyer. He looked at her with his usual lack of expression and said, "Madam Henrietta wondered when you'd be back. Have you reached a decision?"

"Yes," Celia replied with a nod. "I have."

Roland turned his back. "Come along with me, then. I'm sure she'll want to see you."

This time, instead of going through the parlor and up the broad staircase, Roland led her through a small door at the side of the foyer. The door opened into a narrow hall, and there was another staircase, this one strictly functional, at the corridor's end.

Celia and Roland went up the stairs and through another door that opened into the hall she remembered from her previous visit. Without knocking, Roland swung back the door of Madam Henrietta's office and then paused to let Celia precede him. Over Celia's shoulder, Roland said, "Someone to see you, Madam Henrietta."

Celia stepped into the room, trying to control the trepidation she felt dancing around in her belly. At least this time there were no surprises. Madam Henrietta was seated behind her desk, a slight smile on her lovely face, and she was the only one in the office.

"I knew you'd be back," she said to Celia. "What's it going to be, my dear? Are you going to do the sensible thing?"

To Celia, the decision she had reached was extremely sensible, although she knew it wouldn't be to Madam Henrietta. She opened her mouth to explain —

Before Celia could say a word, a scream cut through the air, followed by a huge crash from one of the rooms down the hall. As she jerked around in stunned surprise, the door of the room burst open and a man came stumbling and falling into Madam Henrietta's office.

Celia gasped when she saw his face.

Preston Kirkwood Fox!


Fox was not, by any stretch of the imagination, what was known as a man of the world. Much as he would have liked to think of himself that way, deep down he knew just how inexperienced he really was.

In fact, he had been a virgin until quite recently.

So he was hardly prepared for some of the things that the girl named Melinda demonstrated for him. She obviously had plenty of experience, and a bizarre imagination to go along with it.

Fox let the sensual flow carry him along, hesitating briefly at some of the things Melinda suggested but going along with her in the end.

He lost all track of time, forgot completely about Celia and the real reason he had come here tonight. Instead, he was washed away by a floodtide of passion that left him spent and gasping and wanting only to sleep.

Indeed, he did fall asleep, Melinda's soft warmth snuggled against him in the big fourposter with its luxuriant mattress and silk sheets. Fox slept the sleep of the totally drained—but it didn't last long.

Lips pressed against his with searing heat, and his arms were suddenly full of squirming womanflesh. Fox automatically brought his hands up to caress full breasts with taut, insistent crowns. Deep in the recesses of his brain, something struck him as strange, but he was too busy at the moment to try to identify the anomaly.

"You bitch!"

The shrill cry made Fox's eyes pop open. He found himself looking at extremely close range into Jasmine's face. Her tongue slid insistently into his mouth. On the other side of him in the bed, an angry Melinda tried to reach past him to slap Jasmine.

Fox jerked back from the dark, sloe-eyed girl and gasped, "What are you doing here?"

Melinda squealed, "She's trying to get you away from me, the no-good bitch!"

Jasmine fended off Melinda's blows and tried launching some of her own. "Yellow-haired whore!" she spat at Melinda.

Fox cowered between the struggling women, covering his head as they rained punches and slaps on each other. He was terrified, he discovered, more frightened than when he had been shot at on several occasions.

These two girls were crazy!

He had always had trouble getting one female interested in him, let alone two beautiful concubines such as these. And they were fighting over him!

Mixed in with his fear, Fox felt a sudden surge of pride.

Melinda leaped over him, getting her hands on Jasmine and rolling toward the edge of the bed with the dark-haired girl in a vicious embrace. Fox seized the opportunity and rolled the other way. He leaped up off the bed and lunged for his pants, which were draped over the back of a nearby chair.

Melinda and Jasmine fell off the bed with a thump. They were pulling hair and gouging at eyes now. Jasmine was the smaller of the two, but she possessed a wiry strength that was serving her well. She threw the blond girl off her and struggled to her feet.

As Melinda started to get up, Jasmine caught her under the arms and put all her strength into a heave. Melinda screamed as she tried to catch her balance.

Fox had his pants on by now, and that was as far as he was going to attempt to dress under the circumstances. He headed for the door as Melinda staggered into the dresser with its large, gilt-framed mirror. The impact as the girl slammed into the piece of furniture dislodged the silvered glass.

As the mirror fell with a huge crash, Fox plunged out of the room and into the hall. He wasn't sure where he was going, but he knew he wanted to get away from those two battling spitfires.

A man could get hurt in there!

He saw a door in front of him and slammed it open, looking only for a hiding place. As he lunged into the room, his foot slipped on the carpet and he felt his balance deserting him. He started to fall—

And suddenly there was Celia standing right in front of him, her mouth open in shock.

Celia stared dumbfounded at Fox's sprawled, half-nude form as the young man gabbled, "They're crazy! They're going to kill each other!"

Tearing her eyes away from Fox, Celia glanced over at Roland and saw that the man had reacted automatically to the intrusion. He had a small pistol in his hand, and he had drawn it from under his coat with blinding speed.

Madam Henrietta was on her feet behind the desk now. She rapped at Fox, "Who? Who's going to kill each other?"

"M-Melinda!" Fox exclaimed. "And Jasmine!"

Madam Henrietta struck the top of the desk with a small fist. "Dammit!" she grated. "They know I don't allow fighting between the girls."

Another short scream sounded from down the hall.

Madam Henrietta gestured curly. "Go break it up, Roland," she ordered in sharp tones. "And bring those two bitches back here with you!"

Roland slipped his gun back under his coat and left the room, moving quickly but not hurrying. Celia thought she saw the faintest suggestion of a smile around his thin lips as he went out.

Fox was drawing deep breaths and trying to get to his feet. Celia stepped forward and bent to take his arm. "Let me help you, sir," she said, hoping he would catch the reminder that they were not supposed to know each other.

Fox waved off her offer of assistance and managed to climb upright. He was pale and obviously shaken.

Madam Henrietta came out from behind the desk. "What in the world happened, Mr. Fox?" she asked.

Fox glanced at Celia and looked embarrassed. As well he should, Celia thought.

Madam Henrietta followed his look and reassured him, "Don't worry about Celia here. She's one of my girls, aren't you, Celia?"

Taking a deep breath, Celia started to answer,

but Madam Henrietta had already turned away and was focusing her attention to Fox again.

"I . . . I'm not really sure what happened," Fox began tentatively. "I was with Melinda, as you know, and then I must have fallen asleep . . ." He glanced again at Celia and his skin took on a deeper red flush.

She wished he would stop that! If he wasn't careful, Madam Henrietta might get the idea that they weren't the strangers they were pretending to be.

"And then when I woke up, Jasmine was there, too. She and Melinda started fighting—"

Fox broke off as the door opened and Roland ushered the two girls in question into the room. Both of them were wrapped in silk sheets taken from the bed. Their hair was tousled, and each of them had several bruises and contusions on their lovely features. They glared savagely at each other, but Roland was in between them and had his hands on their shoulders, holding them apart.

Madam Henrietta faced them, furious, and their indignation immediately turned to crestfallen shame. "You girls know I don't allow any displays like this!" the older woman flared at them. "I want an explanation, and I want it now!"

Melinda glanced sullenly at Jasmine. "She came into my room and was in bed with my man. That's reason enough to go after her, isn't it?"

Madam Henrietta swung toward Jasmine. "What about it?" she demanded. "Did you do that?"

Jasmine summoned up her courage and lifted her chin. "What if I did? Judson had his way with me and then went to *sleep,* the worthless old—"

"Enough!" Madam Henrietta hissed. She looked over at Fox, who at the moment seemed intensely interested in the pattern of the carpet beneath his feet. Madam Henrietta went on, "Mr. Fox is a charming young gentleman, but I hardly see what inspired such frenzy on your part, ladies. My apologies for speaking so bluntly, Mr. Fox."

Fox murmured something and shook his head.

Celia couldn't understand it either. The fact that Fox had joined in the celebration arranged by Warren Judson was no surprise, and she supposed it was normal enough that such a party in a place like this would end up in bed. But why would any two women in their right minds fight over Fox?

"He killed those two robbers," Melinda said so softly it was almost a whisper.

"Yes," Jasmine echoed. "He is a brave man."

Oh, Lord, Celia thought. Listening to talk like this would just make Fox's head that much bigger. The young man had grown up some during the mission in Montana Territory, but if this kept up he was going to be the same jackass he had always been before.

Indeed, Fox now had a smile on his face, Celia saw. She repressed a sigh.

"I don't care what reasons you thought you had," Madam Henrietta said. "This house has a

165

reputation to protect, and so do I. There is no fighting here, especially among the inmates. You girls will have to leave."

"No!"

The tortured cry came from both Melinda and Jasmine. No doubt they were seeing in their mind's eye the places where they would probably wind up if they had to leave Madam Henrietta's. There were other parlor houses, but none so elegant as this.

And eventually there would come the cribs and the pigpens, a sordid end if ever there was one.

Madam Henrietta was adamant. She said, "I want both of you packed and out of here within the hour. Roland, see to it that they leave."

Roland nodded his head.

Madam Henrietta turned away, ignoring the sobs and the pleading from her two former employees. As Fox fidgeted, Roland firmly guided Melinda and Jasmine out of the room, shutting the door behind him.

As Madam Henrietta went behind her desk and sat down again with a sigh, Fox said, "I . . . I don't want to interfere—"

"Then don't," Madam Henrietta cut in sharply. "You don't understand about running a business like this, Mr. Fox. There have to be rules, and there can be no exceptions to those rules. One of mine states that there will be no fighting. Those girls knew what they were doing. Now they must pay the price." She put a smile on her face. "But perhaps we can salvage your interrupted evening. There are many other lovely young ladies who would be glad to share your company. Perhaps my newest protégée here . . ."

Celia realized with a shock that Madam Henrietta was referring to her. Quickly, she started shaking her head.

"I'm sorry, Madam Henrietta," she said. "But I've been trying to tell you all evening, I've decided not to accept your generous offer."

The older woman's mouth twisted in disappointment. "You're sure?"

"I'm sure," Celia said.

Madam Henrietta shrugged in resignation. "Well, if you're determined not to do the intelligent thing, Celia, I suppose there's nothing I can do to stop you. But I am sorry you came to this conclusion."

"I'm sorry, too," Celia said, even though she wasn't.

"I'll have Roland show you out as soon as he's through with that other matter."

Celia shook her head. "There's no need. I know my way."

"Very well," Madam Henrietta nodded. She turned her attention back to Fox. "Now, sir, what shall we do to make up for this inconvenience . . . ?"

Celia slipped out of the office as Fox began to smile drunkenly in anticipation.

This evening had been a debacle, for the most

part, but at least she had let Madam Henrietta know that she would not be working at the parlor house. That much would make Landrum and Glidinghawk and, ultimately, Amos Powell happy.

And Fox did seem to be insinuating himself into the inner circle most likely to be behind the plot to discover the commission's findings. So they were making progress on the mission.

But now, Celia suddenly realized, her part of the job was over. She was in the same position Fox had been earlier — no viable cover identity, nothing to do.

Well, she thought with a smile, that would leave her more time for Devlin.

The smile was still on her face as she left the mansion. She wasn't watching behind her, so she didn't see the look that passed between the two men at the front door who let her out.

# CHAPTER FOURTEEN

Despite what the carriage driver had said the first night Celia came here to Madam Henrietta's, there were no carriages in sight along the street. Celia stood for a moment, peering first one way and then the other, trying to decide what to do.

She hoped that while she hesitated, a carriage would come along that she could hire to take her back to the hotel. No such luck, she saw.

Well, there was nothing left for her to do except start back on foot. She certainly didn't want to be late for her dinner date with Devlin. Perhaps a carriage would appear on the street as she walked, and she could hail it then.

Although there were occasional streetlamps, much of the way was dark and shadowy. Celia felt a tingle of nervousness up and down her spine as she set out. Logically, she wasn't worried very much about being bothered. She had a loaded derringer in her bag, and she was good with it. And after all, she was an experienced undercover agent, accustomed to taking care of herself.

But logic did little to allay an instinctive fear of dark places. Celia grimaced and kept walking.

By the time she had gone a couple of blocks, her anxiety had eased somewhat. There were a few other pedestrians out and about—although they were all on the other side of the street—and several men on horseback had ridden by. Celia didn't think anyone would bother her as long as there were other people around.

The hand came out of an alley she was passing. It clamped on her arm and jerked her into a patch of deep shadow.

Celia opened her mouth to scream, but before she could utter a sound, another hand roughly silenced her. The palm of the hand was pressed hard against her lips, and the fingers dug brutally into her cheeks.

An arm went around her waist, pulling her against a man's body. The attacker was large and strong; a small part of Celia's brain that was still rational recognized that much.

For the most part, though, panic leaped and bounded through her, and she shrieked into the muffling hand.

A fist slammed into her belly. Two men, she thought fleetingly, there had to be two of them. Pain doubled her over in the grasp of the first one. He yanked her upright again, and a voice hissed in her ear, "Don't fight us, bitch, and we won't hurt you any more than we have to!"

There was something familiar about the low-pitched voice, but in her terror-stricken state, Celia couldn't even come close to placing it. The man turned away from the street and carried her deeper into the alley.

She was thrown down, landing hard on the floor of the alley and dropping her bag. The breath puffed out of her lungs, leaving her gasping for air and completely unable to yell for help.

One of the men dropped to a knee beside her and grabbed both of her wrists. He leaned forward heavily, pinning her arms down. The other man knelt at her legs and began pulling her dress up. Instinctively, Celia kicked out, and again she was punched hard in the stomach.

"Stop that!" the man beside her legs grated. "Just cooperate, and it'll all be over soon. Who knows, you might even enjoy it, you snooty little baggage."

Tears rolled down Celia's cheeks. She felt herself giving up. They were too strong for her, and she would be better off if she simply went along with what they wanted.

As she blinked away some of the tears, she saw that her vision had adjusted somewhat to the darkness of the alley. She could see her attackers now, and she stiffened with a shock of recognition.

They were the two doormen from Madam Henrietta's. They must have followed her when she left the house, she thought.

It didn't matter who they were. They were going to molest her, and there was nothing she could do about it.

She felt cold night air on her legs. The alley floor was hard and uncomfortable under her head and back. The man holding her arms relaxed his grip somewhat as she went limp beneath him. Her right wrist slipped out of his hand, and the arm flopped bonelessly to the side. Her breathing became shallow.

The man put his hand on her chest in a sudden moment of fear. He was afraid she had stopped breathing, that they had killed her somehow. Murder had never been their intent.

He took a deep breath when he realized that Celia was still alive. Maybe she had just fainted from fear.

Celia was still barely aware of what was going on. She felt her clothes being tugged away from her body and knew, in some part of her mind, what was about to happen. But she had passed the point where she could resist it.

The fingers of her free hand brushed against something.

The nerves in her fingertips recognized the sensation. They were touching the fabric of her bag—the bag containing the derringer.

That message shot through Celia's consciousness, galvanizing her brain out of its defeated state. Suddenly, she lunged to the side, her hand reaching out and delving into the bag, which had come open when it fell. She felt the cold, hard metal of the derringer and closed her fingers on it.

"Look out!" one of the men yelled.

Celia jerked the little weapon out of the bag. She found the trigger as she jammed the muzzle into the side of the man holding her other arm.

He yelled and threw himself to the side just as she pulled the trigger. The derringer cracked wickedly, and the man let out a yelp of pain as the slug burned along his side. It didn't enter his body, though. Instead, it cut a shallow, painful crease in his flesh and then thudded harmlessly into the stone wall of the warehouse on one side of the alley.

Celia had kicked out as she fired the derringer. Her foot thumped into the chest of the other man, knocking him back away from her legs. Seizing the brief chance, Celia rolled across the alley and came unsteadily to her feet, holding the derringer out in front of her and trying to cover the two men, who were several feet apart.

Both of them got to their feet. The one who had been creased held a hand to his wounded side and cursed in pain. The other one massaged his chest, which was aching from Celia's kick, and said, "You shouldn't have done that, girl. We didn't mean to hurt you. We just wanted a little fun."

"But now we're going to kill you, you goddamn doxie!" the other man growled.

"Stay back!" Celia warned them. "I'll shoot."

The wounded man laughed coarsely. "You've only got one bullet left in that popgun, and it won't stop either one of us."

Slowly, they began to advance. Celia swung the derringer back and forth between them as she backed up. The wall of the warehouse stopped her. As the shadowy figures tensed to leap forward at her, she drew a deep breath. She might have time for one scream—

A shape suddenly loomed in the darkness behind the man to Celia's left, the one she had kicked. Someone grabbed the man, spun him around. A fist crashed against his jaw, snapping his head to the side. The man dropped limply, out cold.

The other man said, "Wha—," but that was all he had time for. Major Devlin Henry lunged across the alley at him and slammed into him. Devlin's hands found the man's throat and tightened. He drove the man's head against the wall of the building opposite in a savage attack.

Celia cowered against the wall of the warehouse and watched open-mouthed as the blue-uniformed rescuer disposed of the second attacker. She winced as the man's head struck the wall with a soggy thud. Devlin released the man's throat and stepped back. The man sprawled on the alley floor, and his limp fall signified death.

"Scum," Devlin said quietly, gazing down at the man's body. He was barely breathing hard. Abruptly, he turned, and two quick steps put him at Celia's side. He asked anxiously, "Are you all right?"

She had let the derringer sag to her side when she recognized Devlin. Now it slipped from her fingers entirely as she moved into his arms and buried her face against his broad chest. His arms went around her and tightened in an embrace.

"I'm fine," Celia said, "now."

"They didn't hurt you?"

She was crying again and she knew it, but there was nothing she could do about it. Reaction was really setting in now. For a long moment, she sobbed into his rough blue uniform, then took a ragged breath and said, "They roughed me up a bit, but I'm all right, Devlin, really."

"They didn't . . . ?"

Celia shook her head. "You got here in time to stop that." She leaned back slightly and tilted her face back to look up at him. "What are you doing here? Where did you come from? We weren't supposed to meet until later."

He glanced at the bodies of the two men. The one he had knocked out might be coming to soon. "Let's go somewhere more pleasant to talk," Devlin said. "We can leave these bastards right here."

"That . . . that other one is dead."

"I know." The tone of his voice indicated that

he didn't find that fact particularly distressing. "He was trying to hurt you, so I think he got what he deserved."

Celia found herself unable to argue with that. With Devlin's strong arm around her, they left the alley quickly, putting the violence behind them.

Fifteen minutes later, they were in a small tearoom that was still open even at this hour of the evening. They were the only customers at the moment. The little elderly lady who ran the place had looked somewhat askance at Celia's rumpled appearance, but Celia and Devlin had not let that stop them. Now they each had a cup of steaming tea, and as Celia sipped hers, strength seemed to flow back into her along with the hot beverage.

"Oh, that's wonderful," she exclaimed softly. Although her nerves had settled down somewhat, her hand still shook slightly as she put the cup down on the saucer. "Thank you, Devlin. For the tea . . . and for everything else."

"I'm just glad I arrived in time to help you," he said solemnly. 'What were you doing walking down there in the first place?"

"I could ask you the same question." Although Celia no longer considered him a suspect in the case to which Powell's Army had been assigned, there was something strange in the way Devlin kept turning up.

He sipped his tea, and she could tell he was

trying to put his thoughts in order. Finally, he said, "I was watching you."

"Watching me?" Celia frowned. "Spying on me, you mean?"

Devlin shrugged. "Call it what you will."

"Then you know I went to Madam Henrietta's."

"I know you left there, too. I was going to try to catch up to you when I saw you walking off, but I lost track of you. I suppose when those two pulled you into that alley, it all happened too quickly and I lost sight of you. I was searching all the nooks and crannies in the area when I found you."

Celia's gratitude to him balanced somewhat her resentment that he had been following her. "I went to Madam Henrietta's for a good reason, Devlin."

"I'm sure you did."

"I went there to tell her I was not at all interested in her offer of employment. And I don't expect that I'll ever return to the place again."

A look of relief passed over Devlin's strong face. "That's good to hear," he admitted. "I care for you deeply, Celia."

She reached out and rested her hand on his. "I know. And I feel the same."

Now the proprietor of the tearoom was smiling, the eyes in her wrinkled face twinkling with the knowledge that young love was blossoming in her establishment. She ducked back into the kitchen so that the handsome couple could be alone.

"I'll take you back to your hotel when we're through with our tea," Devlin said. "I don't really feel like eating right now."

Celia nodded. "I'd like that."

She wanted to tell Landrum and Glidinghawk about the mess Fox had gotten into at the parlor house, but that could wait until morning. Both men were probably asleep by now, considering the rough couple of days they had just been through.

When Celia and Devlin had finished their tea, he left a bill on the table and linked arms with her again. This time, as they stepped out onto the sidewalk, good luck arrived in the form of a carriage for hire. The ride back to the hotel was accomplished quickly.

As they entered the lobby, Celia saw that the clerk was not behind the desk. In fact, they were alone in the room. Emboldened by the privacy, she turned to Devlin and said simply, "Come up to my room with me."

He took her hand, twining his fingers with hers. "That's what you want? Honestly?"

Celia nodded.

Devlin bent forward, brushing her lips with his. She leaned closer to him, raising her mouth and kissing him.

"I never refuse a lady's request," he murmured a moment later.

Celia left the lamp off when they entered the room, not out of modesty but simply because it seemed right. Enough light seeped through the gauzy curtains over the window for the two of them to see. Devlin's hands moved gently and deftly, stripping her clothes away until she stood revealed before him, a pale but lovely shadow in the darkness.

She undressed him then, knowing she was being quite bold and daring but wanting this anyway. When he was nude, she moved into his arms, shivering in the exquisite sensation of being enfolded into his embrace.

She felt him picking her up and carrying her to the bed. He put her down ever so gently and lowered himself beside her. His lips found hers again.

The kiss became more urgent, more demanding. Their lovemaking began slowly, even a little tentatively, but soon both of them were lost in each other and the flood of emotion washing over them.

Celia murmured his name, over and over.

The night was long—but not long enough.

# CHAPTER FIFTEEN

"You look downright happy this morning, Celia," Landrum said.

"One might even say satisfied," Glidinghawk added.

Neither man was smiling, but Celia knew they were making fun of her. She blushed furiously, wondering how they had found out that she spent the night with Devlin Henry.

"How I'm feeling isn't important," she told them. "What matters is the mission."

"Of course," Landrum agreed. "And we ought to start making progress soon."

Glidinghawk nodded. "Fox seems to be doing the best of any of us, as much as it pains me to say that. So far Landrum and I haven't turned up much."

"We suspect that either Colonel Porter or that civilian Rainsford might be selling out the commission," Landrum mused. "But we sure as hell don't have any proof. If we could tie either one of them up with Judson or Madam Henrietta . . ."

The three of them were in Celia's hotel room. Even though it was fairly early, the morning sun still slanting in through the window, all of them had already had breakfast. Celia had eaten alone. Devlin had left her room, and the hotel, when the sky was gray with dawn.

"I suppose I'm out of the picture now," Celia said as Landrum lounged against the dresser, his hat in his hand.

The Texan shrugged. "You followed orders. Amos said for you to go to the house and look into the situation. You turned up the connection with Judson, and there were several hints that you could earn extra money by doing something special. They were probably talking about worming information out of any commission members who, uh, purchased your services. I'd say you did a damn good job."

"We'll have to handle it from here, though," Glidinghawk put in.

Celia shook her head, her green eyes flashing. "It's not fair. I'm as much a part of this team as anybody. Why, even Preston has a job now."

"But he didn't at first," Landrum pointed out. "And he was grousing then just like you are now."

Celia's lips tightened. "You're comparing me

with Fox."

"You brought him up," Landrum said flatly. He clapped his hat on his head and stood up straight. "Gerald and I have to get over to the Colorado House. Porter and Rainsford will be waiting for our report."

"And then it'll be back out on another of those expeditions, is that it?"

"Probably," Landrum nodded.

"Fox is already at the bank this morning, carrying out his assignment. And I'm supposed to sit here in this hotel room twiddling my thumbs."

Landrum grinned. "Reckon you and the major can find some way to pass the time. From what I've seen he's not doing a whole hell of a lot of work for the commission. Fact is, I'm not even sure why the army sent him out here."

"Devlin is a very intelligent man," Celia flared. "I'm sure he has a great deal of responsibility."

Landrum glanced shrewdly at her. "You wouldn't be getting serious about him, would you?"

"Why shouldn't I?"

Glidinghawk said in disbelief, "An army man?"

"My father was an army man, remember? My mother was certainly happy with him."

Landrum and Glidinghawk glanced at each other. Obviously, they had known of the romance between Celia and Devlin, but they had been unaware of its seriousness. "You'd best be careful, Celia," Landrum warned her. "There's still something about Henry that strikes me as funny."

"I'm sure I don't know what you're talking about," Celia replied coldly. She had not told either of her partners about the dangerous situation from which Devlin had rescued her the night before. She had broken off the story after telling them about Fox's problems at the parlor house and her own decision not to work there.

If they knew that Devlin had been following her, that fact would probably just make them more suspicious of him.

"Let's go," Landrum said to Glidinghawk. With a last look at Celia's taut, angry face, the two men went out.

When they were gone, Celia sighed heavily and went to the dresser, sitting down in front of it. She halfheartedly began to brush her hair.

She was going to meet Devlin for lunch in a few hours. Until then, she would just have to wait and try not to think about the fact that she was now just a fifth wheel on this mission.

Tom Rainsford was waiting for Landrum and Glidinghawk when they reached the headquarters of the commission. "Ah, I was wondering what had happened to you gentlemen," he said as they were admitted to the commission's suite. He was seated at the big table, documents and maps spread out in front of him.

"We didn't get back in until late yesterday afternoon," Landrum said. "Figured you wouldn't want to be bothered with bad news that late in the day."

Rainsford frowned. "Bad news? Nothing too bad, I hope."

Landrum put his map pouch on the desk and drew out the rough ones that Glidinghawk had made. "We had a little trouble," he said. "These aren't the maps you sent us out with, but they're the best I could do."

Rainsford glanced at the sketched maps and asked, "What happened?"

"Some fellers stampeded our horses to draw us off, then raided our camp and took the real maps," Landrum said. He and Glidinghawk had decided to stick to the truth in this matter. If Rainsford was behind the theft, he would already know what had happened; if he was innocent, telling him the truth wouldn't hurt anything. Landrum went on, "I did the best I could at redrawing the maps from memory. Maybe you can get some use out of them."

Rainsford shook his head for a moment, then said, "Please don't misunderstand, Mr. Davis. I think you did a commendable job under trying circumstances. I was just shaking my head at the misfortune that has seemed to plague this commission. I don't know how much information seems to have been mislaid or disappeared suspiciously since we've started our work. I'm upset about it, and I know Colonel Porter is, too."

"Colonel Porter is what?" The new voice came from the doorway and belonged to the officer in question, Landrum saw as he glanced around. Porter came striding into the suite.

"We've had some more trouble, Colonel," Rainsford said quickly. He explained about the theft of the maps while Porter nodded, a bleak expression on his face.

When he swung to face Landrum and Glidinghawk, he said, "I'm sorry this happened, Mr. Davis. Would you like me to assign a couple of troopers to travel with you and your assistant on your next expedition?"

Landrum shook his head. "That won't be necessary, sir. Now that we know there's a chance of trouble, Glidinghawk and I will keep our eyes open a little better."

"As you wish," Porter said curtly. "Can you start out again today?"

Landrum repressed the sigh of weariness he felt trying to get out. "I suppose we can."

Rainsford put in, "I know this is awfully quick to expect you to undertake another expedition, but I'm afraid Washington is putting some pressure on us to reach a decision."

Porter shot a warning glance at Rainsford. Landrum didn't miss the look. So things were getting tight, he thought. That was interesting. If the commission was under pressure to wrap up their job, that meant the plotters would also have to hurry. Otherwise, the decision would soon be common knowledge, and without advance warning of the new fort's site, the men Powell's Army were after would have no chance to make their illicit fortunes.

Colonel Matthias Porter didn't want word of that pressure leaking out, though. Which could mean anything—or nothing.

Not for the first time, Landrum wished this assignment had been more clear-cut. All this intrigue was damned hard on a man.

Rainsford pushed a sheaf of the army-prepared maps across the table to Landrum. "Those are the areas you need to survey next," he said. "The sooner we get this information, the better. We're very close to reaching a decision now."

Again Landrum saw the sharp glance that Porter gave the civilian. Evidently the colonel believed in keeping his subordinates as much in the dark as possible. Landrum had run into that kind of thinking quite often in the military.

He picked up the maps and stuffed them into his pouch. "We'll get started," he said.

"Try to hang on to those maps this time," Porter snapped.

"We'll try," Landrum replied, carefully keeping his voice flat. No use taking offense—even if the colonel was a dyed-in-the-wool bastard.

They took their leave, striding out of the Colorado House, and turned toward the stable where they had rented horses before.

"Well?" Glidinghawk asked.

"I guess we go back to looking at rocks," Landrum said.

Preston Kirkwood Fox felt like hell.

It wasn't just that he had gotten very little sleep the night before. Nor was it the prodigious amounts of rich food and liquor he had consumed. It wasn't even the strenuous acts of passion in which he had engaged with first Melinda and then another young lady named Jane.

It was all those things combined.

No one had ever told Fox that a life of debauchery was so exhausting—and him still with sore feet!

Still, he reported on time for his day's work at the bank. Although his eyelids were heavy and his eyes themselves were streaked with red, he stayed awake somehow through a morning that seemed to last forever.

Occasionally, his knees would threaten to buckle and his vision would blur. When that happened, he held on for dear life to the counter of his window and waited for the awful sensation to pass.

For breakfast that morning, he had been able to stomach only coffee, and he had had plenty of the strong black brew at the boardinghouse. So far, it didn't seem to have helped him very much.

Warren Judson, on the other hand, seemed disgustingly cheerful this morning. He was his usual hearty, booming self, greeting his employees and customers with laughter when he came strolling in a few minutes after nine. That was his only concession to the previous night's celebration, Fox supposed. The morning before, when Fox first began working at the bank, Judson had been there quite early, before anyone else, according to the guard.

Not long before lunch, Judson came out of his office and over to Fox's cubicle. Fox felt a bit nervous as the banker stood behind him while he completed a transaction with a customer.

The customer, a middle-aged man with the large, hoary hands of a farmer, leaned forward and peered at Fox. "Say, you're that hero feller, ain't you?" he exclaimed with a sudden grin.

Fox tried to smile back, but it came out as more of a grimace. At least a dozen times already this morning, someone had said something to him about the robbery. He was discovering quickly that celebrity wasn't all it was cracked up to be.

"I was just doing my job," he said modestly.

Judson clapped a hand on Fox's back. "No need for such humility, my boy," he said. "You are a hero, after all." His voice dropped as he went on, "Come into my office when you get the chance, Fox."

"Of course, sir."

Judson went back to his office. Fox took care of the other two customers in his line, then rapidly closed his shutter before anyone else arrived. He straightened his coat, ran a hand over his hair, and took a deep breath.

Judson boomed, "Come in!" when Fox rapped on his office door.

"You wanted to see me, Mr. Judson?" Fox said as he closed the door behind him.

"Didn't I just say that five minutes ago?" Judson demanded. "Never mind. Sit down, Fox."

Fox took the seat which Judson indicated, a gnarly-legged armchair in front of the desk.

Judson leaned back in his own chair and put a cigar in his mouth. "Hell of a night, wasn't it?" he grunted.

"Last night?" Fox tried not to groan at the memories. "Yes, sir," he agreed weakly. "A hell of a night."

Judson grinned wider. "Pretty hung over this morning, eh?"

Fox nodded. He winced as Judson opened a drawer in his desk. The drawer squealed in protest as the banker pulled on its handle.

"What you need is a little hair of the dog," Judson proclaimed. He lifted a half-full bottle out of the drawer. "Bourbon all right with you?"

The very thought of drinking liquor right now made Fox want to gag. He tried to swallow his nausea and said, "I . . . I don't believe I'd care for any."

Judson shrugged. "Suit yourself." He took a glass from the drawer and spilled some of the bourbon into it. After tossing off the drink, he licked his lips and said, "Ah."

Fox leaned forward. He wanted to get this interview over with. "If I might be so bold, sir, why did you want to see me?"

Judson squinted at him. "Can I trust you, Fox?"

"Why — of course you can trust me, sir. Didn't I prove that yesterday?"

"You were trying to save your own skin, Fox, and don't try to tell me different. A man like you, in the habit of carrying a gun like that . . . You knew what you were doing, all right, and it wasn't saving my money. But that was the result anyway, and I'm properly grateful. What I'm asking for now is if you want to make some extra money."

Fox felt a surge of excitement. Unless he was mistaken, Judson was trying to recruit him into the effort to discover the commission's decision. He said, "I'm always interested in making money."

"Good," Judson grunted explosively. "I like a man who likes money. I know what to expect from him." He reached into the drawer again and took out a bulky leather pouch. The flap of the pouch was closed and sealed with wax. "I want you to deliver this to Madam Henrietta's for me this afternoon, boy. Can you handle that?"

Fox took the pouch as Judson extended it across the desk. "Of course, sir." He weighed the leather bag in his hands, trying to be unobtrusive about it. It felt like it was full of either documents or money — or both. "But what about my work this afternoon?"

Judson waved a hand. "Don't worry about that.

This is more important. One more thing. Give the pouch to Roland, nobody else. Whatever you do, don't bother Henrietta with it. It's not important enough to disturb her beauty sleep."

Fox nodded. "I'll give it to Roland," he said.

"All right. Run it over there right after you've eaten." Judson took a small stack of bills out of the drawer and slid them part of the way across the desk. "This is for you, for running this errand for me."

Fox had to stand up to reach the money. As he leaned over the desk to pick it up, he was able to glance down and see a little of the inside of the open drawer. He saw a corner of curling parchment with some words scrawled on it.

He recognized the handwriting.

To cover his shock of recognition, Fox scooped up the money Judson was offering him and grinned in pleasure. "This is very generous of you, sir," he said.

"Nonsense. I believe in paying my employees fairly. Now get busy, Fox. You're still working for a living, you know."

"Yes, sir." Fox patted the pouch. "I'll guard this with my life, sir."

"Try not to get into any more gunfights," Judson said dryly.

"Yes, sir."

The smile was still frozen on Fox's face as he left Judson's office. He didn't even go back to his window. Carrying the pouch, he strode out of the bank, anxious to complete Judson's errand.

And wondering how one of the maps stolen from Landrum had wound up in the drawer of Warren Judson's desk. . . .

# CHAPTER SIXTEEN

Fox headed straight for the hotel where Landrum, Glidinghawk, and Celia were staying. The other members of Powell's Army had to know about this development.

They had their proof now that Judson was mixed up in their mission. He must have hired the men who had raided the camp and stolen the maps. Fox wasn't quite sure how to proceed from here, but it seemed logical to him that they should try to get their hands on that map so it could be used as evidence.

There was no answer when Fox knocked on the door of Landrum's room. He went down the hall to Celia's room and rapped on the panel there. His nervousness was growing. What if none of his partners were to be found? That would leave any decisions that had to be made to him.

The door opened, and Celia looked curiously out at him.

As she swung the door back, Celia saw the excitement on Fox's face and wondered what had happened. She stepped back quickly and said, "Come in, Preston."

He slipped into the room and shut the door behind him. "Have you seen Landrum and Glidinghawk?" he asked.

"Not since earlier this morning. What's wrong?"

Fox shook his head. "Nothing. I've got news, though."

Celia felt her own pulse quickening. Her resolve not to think about the case now that her part was over had been severely tested by boredom this morning. She wanted to get involved again, even if it meant working with Fox.

"What is it?" she asked. "Something about Judson?"

"I'd better find Landrum and tell him," Fox muttered. "Do you have any idea where he went?"

"He and Glidinghawk were going to turn in their geological report to the commission," Celia replied. "After that, they were probably going to start on another expedition. They're probably replenishing their supplies and renting horses again."

Fox started to turn away. "I'll try the livery stable. Maybe they're there."

Celia reached out and caught his arm to stop

him. "Tell me, Preston," she insisted. "What did you find out?"

"Well . . ." He hesitated, unwilling to be too rude to Celia. "You remember Landrum talking about that map he wrote, ah, women's names on?"

Celia nodded. "It was one of the maps that were stolen."

"I saw it in Judson's desk a little while ago."

Celia's fingers tightened on his arm. "You're sure?"

Fox nodded. "I saw the writing and recognized it. It was Landrum's scrawl, all right."

Celia saw what that meant just as plainly as Fox did. "This may be the break we need," she said. She released Fox's arm and turned to the wardrobe where her coat was hung. "Come on. We'd better find the others."

"You can't go," Fox said with a frown. "You're not even supposed to know me, let alone Landrum and Glidinghawk."

Celia shook her head. "It doesn't matter. I don't have a cover to protect anymore."

"But they do," Fox pointed out.

Celia stopped as she was shrugging into her coat. A grimace passed over her face. Fox was right, of course. And it was galling that the young man was thinking straighter right now than she was.

With a sigh, she said, "I suppose that's true. It would draw more attention if anyone saw me talking to them. You can probably get away with it, being a man and all."

"That's right. I'll head down to the livery stable immediately."

"If you don't find Landrum and Gerald, you come back here and tell me," Celia said. Realizing that her sharp tone made the words sound too much like an order, she added, "Please."

"Of course," Fox nodded. "As soon as I can. I do have an errand to run for Mr. Judson." He tapped the pouch that he had tucked inside his coat. "I have to deliver this to Madam Henrietta's."

"What is it?" Celia asked.

"I'm not sure. Papers or money or something like that. Maybe even some of the other stolen maps. The pouch is sealed, though, so I can't risk opening it."

"I suppose not." Celia felt a strong sense of curiosity about the package Fox was delivering, but there was no way they could discover its contents without compromising his cover identity.

As he left the room, Celia went to the window and pushed the curtains aside a couple of inches. A few minutes later, she saw Fox emerge into the street below and head toward the livery stable, walking briskly, purposefully.

And she felt the impatience and frustration building inside her. It wasn't fair that she had to stay out of the case for the most part now.

Maybe — just maybe — she was going to have to

pay another visit to Madam Henrietta's.

Fox was lucky. Landrum and Glidinghawk were just coming out of the stable, leading their saddle horses and a couple of pack horses, as Fox hurried up to the large building.

Landrum saw him coming and frowned when it became obvious that Fox intended to speak to them. He glanced over his shoulder and saw that the owner of the stable had gone back into his office, and the hostlers were all busy at the other end of the big barnlike structure. If Fox would just keep his voice down . . .

"I have to talk to you," Fox said as he came up to Landrum and Glidinghawk. Luckily, Landrum thought, the boy had enough sense to be quiet about it.

Landrum gave a short nod. "Not out here in the open," he said. "We'll cut through that alley in the next block. You go the other way, circle back around, and meet us there."

Fox said, "All right," and moved on down the street, not hurrying but not wasting any time either. The entire exchange had been rapid and hushed, and it was doubtful that anyone on the street had even noticed it.

As Landrum and Glidinghawk led the horses toward the alley, the Omaha asked, "What do you think has happened?"

Landrum sighed. "I don't know. I just hope Fox

hasn't done something stupid again." He gave a shake of his head. "Reckon maybe I'm being too quick to jump to that conclusion, but you know how it is with Fox."

"Yes," Glidinghawk said. "Indeed."

They turned in at the narrow alley and proceeded to follow it, pausing when they reached the middle of it. A few moments later, Fox appeared at the opposite end and came toward them, increasing his pace as soon as he was out of sight of the street.

"Who put the burr under your saddle, Preston?" Glidinghawk asked as Fox came up to them, panting slightly. The young man's eyes were big with excitement.

"I found out what happened to at least one of those maps that were stolen from you," he said.

Landrum and Glidinghawk both tensed. "How the hell did you do that?" the Texan asked.

"By doing my job," Fox returned, somewhat stiffly. He was all too aware of how the other members of the team still felt about him sometimes.

"What happened to the map?" Glidinghawk asked quietly, trying to keep them on the subject.

"I saw it in Judson's desk," Fox said. "The way I see it, he's the one who hired those men to rob your camp."

Landrum rubbed his jaw with a calloused hand. "So Judson's got one of the maps, eh? Reckon you could be right, Preston."

"It was the one who wrote your paramours' names on," Fox said. "I couldn't mistake your handwriting, Landrum."

Landrum grinned. "It is pretty ugly, all right," he admitted. "All this does is confirm that Judson is mixed up in what we're investigating. We suspected that already."

"If we had the map as evidence, however, we might be able to get the army to launch a full-scale investigation into his affairs," Glidinghawk said. "Including that parlor house."

Landrum nodded thoughtfully. "We need the map as proof, though."

"That's what I thought," Fox agreed excitedly. "I think I should try to steal it back from him."

Landrum and Glidinghawk both stared at Fox. "Steal it back from him?" Landrum finally exclaimed. "How the devil are you going to do that?"

"I can get into the bank tonight and take it out of his desk," Fox replied. "I'm pretty sure I can get my hands on the keys long enough to make wax impressions of them. The head teller has a set of them, and I can distract him."

"Sounds risky," Glidinghawk mused. "And how do you know that Judson will leave the map in his desk?"

"I don't," Fox admitted. "But even if he doesn't, I'm sure I can come up with some evidence to tie Judson in with Madam Henrietta and the commission."

Landrum frowned and thought for a long moment, then said, "I don't like it. But I don't see what else we can do right now. Time's getting short, and we've got to move while we've got a chance."

"I agree," Glidinghawk said. "I wish things were a bit simpler, but—"

"They'll be simple enough when I get through," Fox broke in excitedly.

"Just be careful," Landrum warned him. "Gerald and I are supposed to be leaving on another of those geological expeditions, but I reckon we'd better stay close instead. We'll go ahead and leave town, just in case anybody's keeping an eye on us, then double back later. We'll be in town again by tonight."

"Excellent. I'll try to get into the bank as soon as it's good and dark." Fox pulled his watch out and glanced at it. "Right now I've got to hurry. I have to deliver a package at Madam Henrietta's for Judson."

"What kind of package?" Landrum asked.

Fox pulled out the pouch and went through the explanation again, and Landrum and Glidinghawk echoed Celia's desire to see what was inside the leather bag. "Damn," Landrum grated. "It's too chancy to open it. But everything we need might be right there in that pouch."

"We'll have the map," Fox assured him. "And pretty soon we'll have enough to hang Judson and whoever his partners are."

"Just don't get killed first," Landrum cautioned him.

"You really think someone would kill over a matter like this?" Fox asked.

"Preston," Landrum said flatly, "I know they would."

During the day, Madam Henrietta's was not nearly as busy as it was at night, but there were still some customers who preferred the daylight hours.

Thick gray clouds had blown in during the noon hour, and now they scudded through the sky, casting a gloomy pall over the city. The air was chilly, and most of the people who were out and about were wrapped tightly in their coats.

A tall man striding toward Madam Henrietta's followed that example. His coat was belted tightly around his waist, and his collar was turned up. A nondescript black hat was pulled down on his graying hair. He kept his bearded face lowered, and no one on the street paid any attention to him.

The man went through the wrought-iron gate and up the flagstone walk to Madam Henrietta's front door. Purposefully, he used the lion's-head knocker to rap on the thick panel. There was only one doorman on duty at this hour, and when he saw who was on the front stoop, he stepped back quickly to admit the man.

"Where's Roland?" the man asked in a low, hoarse voice.

"Upstairs in the office," the doorman answered.

"And Madam Henrietta?"

"Asleep in her room."

"Excellent." The man shrugged out of his long coat, revealing a conservative gray suit. He handed his hat to the doorman, along with the overcoat.

Even in civilian clothes, Colonel Matthias Porter carried himself with a military air. Locking his hands behind his back, he quickly strode through the parlor and headed for the staircase. At the moment, the parlor was empty except for one sleepy bartender who paid no attention to the colonel.

Porter went briskly up the stairs and down the hall to the office. When he knocked, Roland called softly from within, "Come in."

The colonel opened the door and stepped in. His lips were dry with anticipation, and his tongue slipped out to quickly lick over them.

Roland glanced up from the desk and smiled thinly. "Ah, Colonel," he said. "I've been expecting you."

"You're sure Henrietta's asleep?" Porter asked without preamble.

"Quite sure," Roland nodded. "I added a little, ah, insurance to her coffee at breakfast."

"She won't think it unusual that she went to sleep again so soon after getting up?"

"The woman stays up all night, Colonel. She's accustomed to sleeping most of the day."

Porter nodded. He lifted a hand and rubbed his eyes. "You can understand why I worry. With the burden that I have to carry . . ."

"Of course," Roland said smoothly. "It's not easy for a career officer to turn traitor, is it?"

Porter's face flushed with anger. "Damn you," he grated. "I'm not a traitor."

"Perhaps not in the strictest sense of the word. But you are working against the best interests of your country by helping Judson and me find out your commission's decision in advance."

Again Porter passed his hand over his eyes. "I told you all of this . . . this intrigue is not necessary. I've promised to tell you as soon as the commission reaches its decision. There's no need for you to be stealing maps and having your whores pump my staff for information."

Roland leaned back in the chair and steepled his fingers. "Perhaps not, Colonel. But you see, Judson and I don't trust you. You might be capable of double-crossing us. We can't have that. We have our own experts going over all the information gathered by your commission. We'll reach our own conclusions, and if they agree with what you tell us later, we can feel more confident about proceeding with our plans."

"You're referring to your plans to gouge the government for every cent you can manage."

"Exactly." Roland grinned. It was an unusual

show of emotion for the man.

Porter sighed heavily. "All right. We both know you've got me over a barrel. I don't know why I even bother worrying about it."

"That's right, Colonel. You'd do better to concern yourself with the latest little treat we have for you."

Porter's breath began to come faster. "You've found another one?"

"It's not too difficult. The hardest part is making sure that Henrietta knows nothing about it. She loves a dollar, that woman does, but I'm afraid even she has some standards—unlike you and I, Colonel."

"Enough talking," Porter snapped impatiently. "Let's see her."

Roland nodded and got up. He went over to another door and opened it. "Come in here, my dear," he said.

A girl appeared in the doorway and stepped shyly, tentatively, into the room. She wore a bright red dress with a great deal of lace and a neckline low enough to reveal most of her budding breasts. She kept her eyes downcast, the silky blond hair falling in waves around her face. She was not very far out of adolescence.

"Excellent," Colonel Matthias Porter breathed. His face was rapt as he stared at the young girl.

"We guarantee that she's in the condition you require, Colonel," Roland said. He gestured at the long, overstuffed sofa on one wall. "Feel free to use the office. I'll step out for a time and lock the door behind me. And Colonel—enjoy yourself."

As Porter gazed at the girl and saw how she was quivering slightly in nervousness, he knew he would enjoy himself very much.

# CHAPTER SEVENTEEN

Fox didn't recognize the doorman at Madam Henrietta's this afternoon. As the man stared suspiciously at him, he said, "Good day. My name is Preston Fox, and I'm here to see Roland."

The doorman frowned. "You're not here for one of the young ladies?"

"I've come to see Roland on a business matter," Fox replied, allowing some impatience to creep into his voice.

The doorman considered, then stepped back. "Come on in. He may be busy right now, but I'll check."

Fox went into the foyer, grateful to be out of the cold wind. He was not wearing an overcoat, and the chill was slowly creeping into his bones. Now perhaps he would have a chance to warm up.

The doorman disappeared into the parlor for a few minutes, in search of Roland no doubt, Fox thought. He stepped over to the double doors that led into the parlor. At this time of day, the place was almost deserted, although some of the rooms upstairs were probably being put to good use. Fox spotted the bartender and was just about to start in that direction, anticipating a brandy to warm him up, when Roland appeared on the staircase.

"Good afternoon, Mr. Fox," Henrietta's right-hand man said. The doorman was following along behind him. Roland went on, "What can I do for you today?"

Fox moved closer to Roland while the doorman went back to his post. In a low voice, Fox said, "I have some business to conduct with you, sir. Could we perhaps go up to the office?"

"I'm afraid the office is being used at the moment."

That was strange. Judson had implied that Madam Henrietta would be asleep at this time of day. What was she doing in the office?'

That was none of Fox's business, though. He had his orders to carry out. Tapping the pouch through his jacket, he whispered, "Mr. Judson sent me over with something for you."

Roland nodded. "Ah, yes. Perhaps we should go upstairs." He turned and started up the stairs without waiting to see if Fox was following him.

Fox was. He followed Roland to a much smaller office, where he handed over the pouch. Roland took it and opened it, tearing the wax seal loose. He seemed unconcerned that Fox was still in the room, so Fox took the opportunity to try to sneak a look inside the bag.

As he had suspected, he saw not only papers but several packets of currency also. "Very good," Roland muttered to himself as he thumbed through the contents of the pouch. He extracted one of the bills and extended it to Fox. "I don't know if Judson has already paid you for this errand, Fox, but a little extra loyalty won't hurt."

"Indeed not." Fox grinned. He took the money and put it in his pocket, looking for all the world like a greedy sycophant anxious only to advance himself.

It wasn't much of an acting job, he thought wryly. Not too long ago, that was exactly what he had been.

"I have a feeling we'll be seeing a great deal of you around here, Mr. Fox," Roland said.

"I hope so," Fox replied sincerely. "I could grow to like this place."

Roland made a small noise.

Fox realized half an hour later, when he was back at his duties at the bank, that the man had been laughing.


Night came early at this time of year in Denver, but it couldn't have come too soon to suit Preston Fox.

The afternoon had been a long one. He could barely keep his mind on his work for thinking

211

about the daring mission that night would bring.

In the middle of the afternoon, old Boswell, the head teller, had taken a break just as Fox had expected him to. Boswell had a set of the bank's keys, and despite all his earlier talk about efficiency, he also had a fondness for the whiskey he carried in a small flask in his pocket. While Boswell slipped out the back door to take a nip, it was simple for Fox to step around the partition between windows and take the keys from Boswell's drawer.

Fox had been prepared. The guard at the back door couldn't see anything from his post. Nerves made Fox's hand shake somewhat, but he was able to take impressions of the keys using the wax he had purchased after his visit to Madam Henrietta's. Then he had returned the keys to their proper place and stepped back to his window just as Boswell came in the back door.

Finding a locksmith to file copies of the keys had been a bit more difficult, but Fox had managed that, too, after his day's work at the bank was over. He had finally located a small locksmith shop whose owner was willing to engage in dubious activities as long as several bills crossed his palm.

Now, armed with his illicit keys, Fox was crouched at the back door of the bank, trying to make one of them work on the lock.

The air blowing through the alley was still cold. Fox was worried that it might start to snow or sleet, although it was still a little early in the season for that. Still, at these elevations, almost anything was possible. Fox shivered as he tried another of the keys.

The lock clicked open.

He felt like cheering, but he restrained the impulse. There were no guards on duty in the bank at night—all the cash was locked up in the massive vault—but there was no point in risking drawing attention to himself.

It wasn't money he was after. All he wanted was a good look through Warren Judson's desk.

It was a good thing Landrum and Glidinghawk were being forced to lie low by their circumstances. If they had been able to operate openly right now, instead of having to pretend to be out of town, they would be here with him, prepared to steal any thunder that might arise.

Instead, he, Preston Kirkwood Fox, who had been ignored and banished to a squalid boardinghouse at the beginning of this case, was going to be the one to crack it wide open. Coming on the heels of his successes in Montana, this was going to confirm his position as an important cog in the machine that was Powell's Army.

Soon, no one would ever be able to look down on him again.

Why, he might even get his uniform back.

Fox carefully closed the bank door behind him. A little light filtered into the building through the front windows, and he was familiar with its layout from his two days working here. Moving quickly but cautiously in the shadows, he made his way past the tellers' windows to the door that led into Judson's office.

The office door was locked. Fox worked by feel, trying one key after another until one worked. The door gave a creak as Fox opened it, and he flinched at the sound. But there was no one in the bank to hear it except him.

As he closed the office door behind him, he squinted into the darkness. There was only one window in this room, and it was heavily curtained. He decided he could take a chance on lighting the lamp on the desk.

Taking a match from his pocket, he felt around until he had the lamp located. Then he scratched the lucifer into life on the sole of his boot, as he had seen Landrum do many times. Fox gave a little laugh of jubilation as the match flared.

He held the flame to the lamp's wick until it caught. As the warm glow spread through the room, Fox replaced the chimney and turned toward the desk's drawers. He hoped they weren't locked. It wasn't likely that Boswell would have had the keys to the drawers among his set of keys.

Again Fox's luck held. None of the drawers were locked, including the big one in the middle where he had seen the map earlier. Now, as he slid it open slowly to avoid any excess noise, he peered into it, hoping to see the parchment again.

There were no maps in the drawer.

Fox tried to swallow his disappointment. It would have been too much to hope for, he told himself, to find the map that easily. Perhaps it was in one of the other drawers. He bent over to open the bottom one.

"Just stay right where you are."

The voice came from the doorway. Fox had been so absorbed in his search that he hadn't heard it opening. He jerked upright, despite the command to be still, and stared into the muzzle of a pistol.

The weapon was in the hand of Warren Judson, and the banker's expression was colder than the Colorado night outside.

"Something told me I couldn't trust you, Fox," Judson went on. "I didn't really expect you to try something this soon, though."

The banker's usual joviality had vanished. He looked as if the only thing that would make him happy at this moment would be to blow a hole right through Preston Kirkwood Fox.

Fox tried to find his voice. "You . . . you d-don't understand, sir," he faltered. "This isn't what it looks like."

"It looks to me like you were rifling my desk," Judson grunted. "I'm glad I was passing by and decided to look in for a moment. Lucky for me. Unlucky for you." The banker frowned thoughtfully. "But why didn't you go for the vault? There's no money in here—"

He broke off suddenly, his eyes widening as

another possibility obviously occurred to him.

Fox's hands were raised. He took a step back against the wall as Judson advanced toward him.

"Please, sir. You know you can trust me. I saved your money from those robbers . . . !"

"Shut up," Judson grated. "You're no simple thief, I'll give you that. You wormed your way into my confidence for a reason, though, and I think I know why."

Fox shook his head. "I don't know what you're talking about, Mr. Judson."

"We'll see."

Judson was close now, only a couple of feet away, and Fox frantically tried to decide whether he should try to jump the man. Maybe he could wrestle the gun away from him — but Judson was so big. . . .

Judson didn't give Fox a chance to debate his course of action for long. He lashed out with the hand holding the gun. Fox tried to duck, but his reaction was too slow.

The gun barrel thudded into the side of Fox's head.

Fox's involuntary cry was cut short by the impact. He slumped back against the wall, his knees buckling, and then pitched forward onto his face. He was vaguely aware of his cheek hitting the rug on the floor of the office. The rug scraped his skin —

And then for a time, Fox felt nothing at all.

\* \* \*

In addition to the front and side doors of Madam Henrietta's, there was also a back door. A path led from the alley behind the mansion to this entrance.

Not long after the disaster that had befallen Fox inside the bank, a bulky figure came up that rear walk carrying someone over his shoulders. It was quite dark back here, but the man hauling his human burden was very familiar with the path. He trudged up to the door and knocked sharply on it.

A few moments later, Roland opened the door, a gun in his hand, and then stepped back in surprise as light from inside spilled out on the newcomers. "What the hell?" he exclaimed.

"I caught this young bastard in my office," Warren Judson replied. "I think we'd better have a long talk with him and find out just how much he knows."

Roland nodded. "Yes, I think you're right. Bring him in."

The banker disappeared inside the house, and Roland shut the door.

Once again the small rear yard of the house was quiet and deserted. Several minutes passed, and then there was suddenly motion in the darkness. A darker patch of shadow moved away from the house and slowly made its way toward the alley.

The watcher had seen and recognized Judson and Fox in that brief moment of illumination. This was an unexpected disruption of his plans.

He had suspected Judson from the first of being involved in the mess that had brought him to Denver, but what the devil did Fox have to do with it all?

The shadowy figure reached the alley and moved more quickly now. The man's mind was working feverishly. He had no doubt that Roland and Judson would kill Fox if they had to.

He couldn't let an innocent man die—and he certainly had no knowledge that Fox was guilty of anything. But to act now would ruin his cover and possibly negate everything he had done.

He had no choice, he suddenly decided. But if he was going to throw caution to the winds, there was something he had to do first.

The hurrying figure passed under a streetlamp that was guttering in the sharp wind. The faint glow revealed a man in high black boots, pulled-down hat—

And the uniform of a major in the United States Army.

# CHAPTER EIGHTEEN

When the sharp knocking came on her door, Celia expected to see Landrum or Glidinghawk or even Fox when she opened it.

She didn't expect to find Major Devlin Henry standing there in the hall, his handsome face set in tight, grim lines.

"Devlin!" Celia exclaimed. "Were we supposed to see each other tonight? I don't remember—"

Devlin shook his head and cut in, "We didn't have anything planned. But something important has come up, and I've got to talk to you, Celia."

"Of course. Come in."

Celia stepped back to admit him to the hotel room and didn't bother trying to hide her frown of puzzlement. Devlin was attached to the commission. Could something have happened that was going to take him away from Denver? His expression was certainly bleak, as if what he had to tell her was not good news.

As Celia closed the door, Devlin stood tensely in the center of the room, his hat clutched tightly in his hands. He swung to face her and said bluntly, "I've lied to you, Celia."

Her breath seemed to catch in her throat. "Lied to me? How could you have lied to me, Devlin? You mean . . . about us?"

"In a way. I've certainly lied to you about myself. I wasn't sent here just to be a minor functionary on the commission staff."

Celia's pulse began to speed up as she sensed the seriousness of what he was saying. "Are you trying to tell me you're not a major in the army?"

"Oh, I'm a major, all right. But I was sent to Denver by General Carruthers back in Washington City to investigate reports of corruption on the commission. I guess you could say I'm a kind of undercover operative."

Celia tried not to stare. There was a strange queasy feeling in the pit of her stomach.

And at the same time, there was a part of her that wanted to laugh and laugh. . . .

Her mind was racing. So Devlin Henry was a agent working on the same case that had brought her here. That didn't mean he knew anything about Powell's Army. In fact, it was highly likely that he had no idea other operatives were already on the scene.

She forced down the impulse to tell him the truth—all the truth this time. Amos Powell had drummed the need for secrecy into them, especially when they were dealing with the military. Revealing her real identity to Devlin might ultimately mean the disbanding of the group. It was impossible to say what the long-term results might be.

"Why are you telling me this?" she asked.

"Because I couldn't keep it a secret any longer. I'm tired of having to lie to you, Celia, or at least hold back the whole truth. I started out keeping an eye on you not only because I was interested in you—but because I thought you might be involved in the case I'm working on."

"I was a suspect?" she said incredulously.

Devlin shrugged. "You were at Madam Henrietta's, and that seems to be the center of the plot I was investigating. It so happens that Henrietta really was married to me. That's why General Carruthers picked me for this job. I haven't always been a . . . a spy. The general knew I could get in to see her, though."

"So that's why you kept turning up. You were following me as part of your job." Celia couldn't keep a certain degree of coolness out of her voice.

Devlin tossed his hat on the bed and stepped closer. His hands reached out and grasped her upper arms. "It's worse than that. I even hired a man to search your room and try to find out if you were someone other than who you had told me. It was awful of me to do that, I know—especially when—I found myself—coming to care for you," he said intently. Staring into her eyes, he went on, "The things I told you when we were alone . . . those were the truth, Celia. I swear."

His mouth came down on hers, hot and insistent and urging, and Celia felt her anger and resistance fading. She sagged against him, letting his arms go around her and fold her tightly to him.

They stood that way in the center of the room for what seemed like a long time. The part of Celia's brain that was not carried away by passion was feverishly considering the implications of this development. There had to be something that Devlin hadn't told her yet.

When the kiss finally ended, she put her face against his chest and said softly, "Why now? Why tell me all this tonight?"

One of his hands lightly stroked her back and then reached up to brush her silky red hair. "Because I'm going to have to do something that will end my effectiveness as an agent. I'm going to have to come out into the open, and it may be dangerous."

Celia felt a cold fingertip edging along her spine. "You're going to confront Henrietta with your suspicions?"

"It's worse than that. They're holding a prisoner there at the house. I don't know what his connection is, but I overheard enough to know that they're planning to torture him. I can't let them do that. I've got to try to rescue him."

A horrible premonition raced through Celia's brain. "Who . . . who is this man?"

"You remember hearing talk about an attempted robbery yesterday at one of the banks downtown? The teller who prevented the theft and killed a couple of the robbers is a man named Fox. He's the one being held prisoner. Like I said, I have no idea what he has to do with the case, but his boss, Warren Judson, is involved up to his neck—"

Devlin broke off when he realized Celia was shuddering. "What is it? What's wrong?"

Damn Preston Fox, Celia thought. He must have gotten caught in Judson's office, and now because of his carelessness, Devlin was going to have to risk his life in a rescue attempt.

But there was no doubt in her mind that Fox would die if someone didn't help him.

"I . . . understand what you have to do," Celia said. "But please be careful."

Devlin cupped her chin and tilted her head back. He smiled down at her. "You can bet on that. Still, I had to see you before I go in there, just in case—"

Celia put a finger on his lips. "Don't say it."

He shook his head. "I've got to. I couldn't have all the lies and secrets between us any longer. I don't know what the future will bring, Celia, but I wanted you to know that what we've had here . . . was real."

She buried her face against his chest again. "I

know," she murmured, "I know."

Devlin held her for a moment longer, then released her and picked up his hat. "I have to get back there," he said, not even looking at Celia now for fear that his resolve would shatter. He slipped his army Colt from its holster and checked the loads in its cylinder, an act which sent another cold chill through Celia with its grim meaning. "I've waited too long already."

He settled his hat on his head and went to the door, pausing only long enough to cast one last glance at her over his shoulder. Then he was gone, the door shutting softly behind him.

Celia stood there for only a moment, and then she reached for her coat. Fox was her teammate, and Devlin was . . . Well, Devlin was important to her.

If there was anything she could to to help both of them, she was damn well going to do it.


Landrum and Glidinghawk had ridden out from Denver during the afternoon, heading west. They had kept a sharp eye on their backtrail as they gradually curved to the south. The Omaha had good eyes, as did the Texan, and both men were experienced in these matters.

They would have been willing to bet that no one was following them.

Late in the afternoon, Landrum had said, "We'd better be heading back."

Glidinghawk nodded. "Fox has learned a great deal, but I still have a bad feeling about this, Landrum."

"You and me both," Landrum agreed grimly. He put the spurs to his mount and kicked it into a loping run to the northeast, toward Denver.

Even though they had ridden fairly hard, it was still after dark before they reached the city. They dropped the pack animals off at the livery stable but kept the saddle horses. Riding through the alley behind Judson's bank, they saw that the place was dark and appeared deserted.

"Well, at least he didn't blow the place up," Landrum grunted. "After what he did to that mountain up in Montana Territory, I was afraid he might've taken a liking to dynamite."

Glidinghawk dropped silently out of the saddle and tried the back door of the bank. "Locked," he said. "Maybe Fox hasn't even been here yet."

"That's possible," Landrum allowed. "Come on. We'll go back to the hotel and see if Celia's heard from him."

After riding through the back alleys to the hotel, they left their horses tied up where the animals wouldn't be noticed, then slipped up the rear stairs. The two of them had just reached the second floor and started down the hall when the door of Celia's room opened hurriedly.

She came out into the hall and stopped abruptly as she saw them. Landrum noted the worried lines on her features and the expression of relief that passed over her face when she spotted them coming toward her.

Something was wrong, damned wrong.

He strode forward and put his hands on her shoulders. "What is it?" he asked.

"Fox has been captured. He's at Madam Henrietta's with Judson. They're going to torture him to find out who he is and how much he knows."

The words came spilling out of Celia. Glidinghawk's breath hissed out between gritted teeth, and trenches appeared in Landrum's lean cheeks as his face grew taut. "How the hell did you find out all of this?" the Texan asked.

"Devlin Henry told me."

Glidinghawk frowned. "That army major you're sweet on? What's he got to do with any of it?"

Celia laughed, but there was no humor in the sound. "He's an undercover operative for some general back in Washington. He was sent here on the same mission as we were."

Landrum gave a small shake of his head as he tried to absorb that surprising piece of information. "Does Henry know about us?" he asked.

"He certainly didn't seem to," Celia replied. "He's going to try to rescue Fox, but he . . . he wanted to see me first and tell me the truth. He's in love with me, I think."

"Yeah, well, we'll worry about that later," Landrum grunted. He realized he was still holding Celia's shoulders. He let her go and stepped back. His hand went to the walnut grips of his .44. He slipped the gun out and spun the cylinder to check the cartridges in the weapon, unconsciously copying Devlin's earlier action. Glidinghawk was doing the same thing.

"How long ago was the major here?" the Omaha asked.

"He just left a few minutes ago." Celia looked at both of her partners and went on, "We've got to help him. We've got to try to get Fox out of there.

Landrum nodded. "Reckon you're right. But I'd like to keep our real identities a secret, too, if we can. Glidinghawk and I will work out some kind of story on the way over to Madam Henrietta's."

"What about me?"

"You're staying right here," Landrum told her flatly.

Celia's temper flared. "The hell I am! I'm part of this team, too, Landrum Davis, even though you seem to forget that at times. I've been shot at just as much as you and Gerald!"

"That's nothing to brag about," Glidinghawk pointed out dryly.

"And you're still not going," Landrum added.

Celia opened her bag and drew out a small revolver. "We're wasting time," she snapped. "I'm going, and that's all there is to it." She thought feverishly in an effort to find a reason that would convince Landrum. "If we can catch up to Devlin, I can tell him that I ran into the two of you and told you about what's happening because you work for the commission. You can offer to help him rescue Fox."

"Why should he trust us?" Landrum asked. "He doesn't know us."

"But he does know and trust me," Celia pointed out. "Besides, he knows that you two came to Denver on the same train he did. How could you be part of the trouble when you just got here?"

Landrum nodded thoughtfully. "Might work," he allowed. "I guess it's worth a try. But you lie low when we get there."

Celia nodded. She was willing to agree to almost anything at the moment if they could just get moving.

"Come on," Landrum said. "We've just got the two horses, but I guess you can double up with me."

Celia smiled and put the gun back in her bag. She kept her fingers clenched around the butt of it, though, as they hurried downstairs and out into the alley.

Landrum and Glidinghawk mounted up, and then Landrum reached down to give Celia a hand. She grasped his wrist and swung herself onto the horse's back behind the saddle.

"Hang on tight," Landrum told her. "We've got to hurry."

Celia nodded, leaning against his back and putting her arms around his middle. She locked her hands together as Landrum kicked the horse into a gallop.

They rode out of the alley and around to the street that ran in front of the hotel. Celia could feel her heart pounding in her chest as she held on to Landrum. The beat of her pulse seemed as loud as the drumming of the horses' hooves on the hard-packed dirt of the street.

She prayed they would catch up to Devlin in time. If he went in there alone, one man against who knew how many well-armed foes . . . and among them the cold-eyed killer called Roland —

Celia shivered and held on tighter to Landrum.

# CHAPTER NINETEEN

Major Devlin Henry gave a friendly grin to the man who admitted him to Madam Henrietta's. He recognized the man from his previous visit, and the doorman seemed to remember him as well.

"Good evening," Devlin said. "I'd like to see Madam Henrietta."

"Of course, sir. I believe she's in the parlor."

Devlin kept smiling to hide his disappointment. He wanted to get upstairs, because that was probably where Fox was. He had assumed that Roland would be summoned to escort him to Henrietta's office, and as soon as they were in the upstairs corridor, Devlin had planned to jump Roland and knock him out.

It wasn't going to work out that way. So he would just have to make the best of it, he told himself.

He went on into the parlor. There were fewer customers tonight than on his earlier visit, perhaps because the colder weather was keeping some folks at home. But there were still plenty of happy people in the big room.

Devlin spotted Henrietta near the bar and began threading his way through the crowd toward her. She saw him coming and smiled. To look at her, he thought, you wouldn't know that she had anything to hide.

"Good evening, Devlin," she said as he came up to her. "I really didn't expect to see you back here."

"I had to come see you again," he replied, trying to decide what tack to take with her. Appealing to her greed would probably be the best course. "I have some business matters to talk over with you."

Henrietta frowned prettily. "What sort of business could you and I possibly have, Devlin? I thought the divorce decree had severed all of our ties."

"Except a certain amount of friendship," Devlin amended, and he was surprised to find that he was telling the truth. There was a part of him that was still fond of Henrietta. He went on, "Could we go upstairs to your office and discuss it?"

She shrugged her bare shoulders. "I suppose so. I'm not needed down here at the moment. Come along."

She carried herself with a certain imperiousness, he thought as he followed her up the broad staircase. And her beauty was undeniable. It was a shame she had never been able to resign herself to being the wife of a military man.

God, how he had loved her!

But that was all over now. If she was involved in the plot he was investigating, he would do his best to bring her to justice, just as if he had never met her before.

When they reached her office, Henrietta strolled in and left the door open. She went behind the desk but didn't sit down. "Now," she said, "what are these business matters you need to discuss with me, Devlin?"

He glanced around the room. "Where's Roland?"

Henrietta waved a hand. "Oh, he's around somewhere, I assume. Why?"

"I just thought you'd like to have him here."

She laughed shortly. "I assure you, my dear, I can handle my own affairs without some man to hold my hand." Her tone became more impatient. "What was it you wanted?"

"This," Devlin said.

His fist shot across the desk, catching her on the point of the jaw. He pulled the punch somewhat, but there was still enough power in it to snap her head around. Henrietta didn't make a sound. Her eyes rolled up in her head and she slumped to the floor behind the desk.

Devlin grimaced as he leaned over the desk to

make sure she was unconscious. Despite what had happened between them in the past, he hadn't enjoyed that.

Henrietta certainly hadn't acted as if she knew a man was probably being tortured under her roof at this very moment. Devlin suddenly wondered if he could have been wrong about her.

There was too much evidence pointing to this house as the center of the plot against the commission. She had to be part of it, he thought. Or did she?

Devlin's eyes narrowed in thought. From what he had seen of Roland, the man was capable of almost anything. Could he have been working behind Henrietta's back?

There would be time to sort that out later. Right now he had to find Fox.

Devlin unsnapped the flap of his holster and slid his Colt out as he went into the hall. Walking quietly, he went to the doors of the other rooms along the corridor. The doors were fairly thick, but not so thick that he couldn't hear sounds coming from the rooms that were occupied.

From several of the rooms came the unmistakable noises of lovemaking. Devlin passed them by and concentrated on the rooms from which no sounds emanated. Finding the doors unlocked, he jerked them open and went in quickly, his gun ready.

The rooms were as empty as they had sounded from outside.

That left the third floor. Devlin went to the rear

stairs this time, ducking around a corner just as one of the house's customers, accompanied by a girl, came up the stairs to the second floor. He catfooted his way up the stairs to the third floor.

The same lack of results awaited him there.

All the rooms up here were empty at the moment, although no doubt they would be in use before the evening was over. Devlin found a shadowy corner and stood there for a moment, trying to decide what to do next.

So far, his daring rescue attempt had fallen flat on its face. All he had managed to do was clout Henrietta. He was no closer to locating Fox.

Unless . . .

He returned to the narrow rear stairs and saw that they led up one more flight. It was possible, given the construction of the house, that there was at least one room in the attic. He would check up there, and then if that didn't pan out, all that would be left was the basement.

The basement would be harder to reach without anyone spotting him. With his hopes centered around the attic, Devlin started up the stairs.

They ended in a small landing. A dark corridor led away from the landing, and at the far end of the hall was a door. Devlin could discern its outlines because a light was burning on the other side of it, casting a faint glow through the cracks around the door. He started in that direction, tightly gripping his revolver.

As he crouched outside the door, he was rewarded by the sound of a fist smacking into flesh, followed by a low moan. A voice said, "Give it up, Fox. You might as well tell us who you're working for. We'll find out in the end anyway."

Devlin recognized the booming tones of Warren Judson.

He grasped the knob, twisted it abruptly, and thrust the door open. As it banged back against the wall of the attic room, Devlin stepped through the entrance, pointing his gun right at Judson's startled, beefy face.

"Hold it!" Devlin rapped.

His eyes flicked around the room, taking in the scene. Judson and another man, one of the hefty doormen, were standing in front of a ladder-backed chair. Preston Fox was tied into that chair, and his face bore the marks of a beating. So far, though, that seemed to be all they had done to him.

"What the hell!" Judson exclaimed.

And then Devlin stiffened as a cold ring of metal pressed into the back of his neck. Roland said quietly, "Please don't move, Major, or I'll have to blow your spine in two."

Devlin felt his heart sinking. He had let Roland sneak up on him, and now he and Fox would probably both die in this dusty little room. Some undercover agent he had turned out to be!

"What is this, Roland?" Judson demanded.

"I'd say the major here is not what he appears to be," Roland said. "Go on inside, Major, and we'll discuss it. But drop that pistol first."

Devlin let the Colt fall to the floor. He hoped the impact would make it discharge and draw some attention to his plight, but that didn't happen.

As Devlin stepped into the room, Fox opened his eyes and tried to lift his lolling head. Devlin saw the hope there in Fox's eyes, the prayer that someone had come to save him—

And then he saw that hope die.

One of the doormen put out an arm and barred Glidinghawk's way. "No Injuns allowed in here, mister," he said to Landrum. Then, taking in Landrum's dusty range clothes, he went on, "And you don't look much like the type we cater to either."

"I've got money," Landrum snapped. "And the Indian goes where I go."

The doorman squinted at Landrum. "Say, don't I remember you from a few nights ago? You got drunk and we had to toss you out. You haven't come back to make trouble, have you, ace?"

Landrum shook his head. "No trouble."

A Winchester suddenly erupted into life somewhere behind the house, blasting away in a roll of gunpowder thunder.

Landrum jerked his .44 from its holster and cracked the doorman alongside the head with the barrel.

Shoving the suddenly unconscious doorman aside, Landrum bounded through the foyer and into the parlor, Glidinghawk at his heels. Several of the house's girls screamed.

One thing about Celia, Landrum thought fleetingly. When she gave a signal, she didn't do it halfway.

Their desperate ride through the night hadn't been fast enough to let them catch up to Devlin Henry. They had been close enough to see him enter the house, however, and since then had been busy coming up with a plan. Celia had been left in the alley behind the house with a Winchester to provide a distraction while Landrum and Glidinghawk went in the front door.

Gunfire broke out in the house now, upstairs somewhere. Landrum caught Glidinghawk's eye and jerked his head toward the staircase. Shoving men aside, they made their way to it and started up.

Two of Madam Henrietta's men appeared at the top of the stairs, guns in hand. Both of them snapped shots at the intruders.

Landrum went to one knee as a slug shrieked close by his ear. He triggered the Colt and saw one of the men go spinning away with a shattered shoulder. Beside him Glidinghawk fired and dropped the other one.

Then the Omaha was bounding up the stairs, Landrum right behind him.

Well, they had never intended the plan to be

really subtle, Landrum thought.

Simply put, they were here to bust hell out of the place and pick up the pieces later.

As the cracking of the Winchester reached the attic room, Roland half turned in surprise. That pulled the barrel of his little pistol away from Devlin Henry's neck.

He'd never get a better chance, and he knew it.

Devlin drove an elbow back, slamming it into Roland's chest. Roland was much lighter than Devlin, and the blow sent him staggering hard into the wall of the room.

Devlin whirled, lashing out with an arm. He hit Roland's wrist and knocked his gun hand aside. Devlin sunk his other fist in the slender man's belly.

A weight fell on Devlin from behind as the doorman jumped him. Devlin staggered, trying to keep his balance. With a roar, Judson started forward to get into the fracas.

Preston Fox summoned up strength from somewhere to rock his chair back and forth. As he lunged against the ropes that bound him, the chair suddenly fell, spilling him in front of Judson. The banker's legs became tangled in the unexpected obstacle, and he went sprawling.

Gasping for breath, Roland recovered his balance and brought his pistol up and jerked its barrel toward the struggling figures. He triggered it twice just as Devlin wheeled around, the doorman still trying to strangle him from behind.

Roland's bullets thumped into the doorman's back, making him stiffen. Devlin heard him grunt once in pain, and then the strangling hands went away as the man fell to one side.

Devlin turned again and found himself staring into the barrel of Roland's gun. Above it, the man's pale face was set in cold, murderous lines.

The chair in which Fox had been tied had broken when Judson's bulk fell on it. Fox twisted desperately in his ropes, trying to get out of the entanglement. As Judson struggled to his feet, Fox reached behind him with his bound hands and caught up one of the broken chair legs. Fox lunged, thrusting out blindly with the leg of the chair.

The leg went between Judson's ankles and tripped him again. In the small confines of the room, Judson fell forward, crashing into Devlin and knocking him aside just as Roland pulled the trigger again.

"Goddamn!" Roland screamed as he saw Judson's head snap back, a small, black-edged hole appearing on the banker's forehead. Blood began to well from the hole as Judson fell lifelessly to the floor.

"You won't be so lucky again!" Roland panted in fury as he covered Devlin and Fox. "I'll kill you both!"

"Hey!" a voice yelled from the other end of the

hall.

Roland spun and saw a tall man standing there, a man with a gun in his hand. Another man appeared behind the newcomer.

All of Roland's carefully structured plans had suddenly fallen apart, for no apparent reason. Now, in this little room filled with the smell of gunpowder and blood, he saw his own ruin.

And he wasn't going to go down alone.

He jerked the gun up and his finger tightened on the trigger.

Landrum Davis and Gerald Glidinghawk fired at the same instant. Their bullets slammed into Roland's thin chest, pulping flesh and bone and flinging him backward in a bloody sprawl.

He died with a grimace on his face, his eyes wide open behind shattered spectacles.

With Glidinghawk covering the rear, Landrum strode down the hall and looked into the room, his Colt ready to fire again. He took in the bodies of Roland, Judson, and the doorman, then glanced at Devlin. "You all right?" he asked.

"Yes, I am," Devlin said, not quite believing it yet. He and Fox had been rescued from certain death, but by whom . . . ? "Don't I know you?"

"Landrum Davis," the Texas introduced himself. "And this is Gerald Glidinghawk behind me. We came into town on the same train as you. We've been doing geological surveys for that commission you're assigned to."

"But why . . . how . . ."

Landrum grinned. "We'd best get out of here, all of us. And then there's a little lady downstairs who'll explain all of it to you."

Somehow, without being told, Devlin knew who Landrum was talking about.

*Celia.*

# CHAPTER TWENTY

Landrum had left enough shells with Celia for her to reload the Winchester once she had emptied it to provide a distraction. She was supposed to wait here in the alley and let Landrum and Glidinghawk handle things inside.

But now, as she fed fresh cartridges into the rifle's magazine, she knew she couldn't do that.

Not with Devlin inside and probably in danger.

She wasn't sure how she felt about the man now. His revelation that he was working undercover had put a subtly different cast on their relationship. And yet, he hadn't done anything that she herself had not done.

Celia wasn't going to worry about that now. All she wanted at the moment was to wrap this mission up.

She spotted the rear door of the mansion and ran toward it. The door was locked, she discovered when she got there, but a .44 slug through the lock took care of that. She jerked it open and hurried through.

Celia hadn't been in this part of the house before, but it was easy enough to find the parlor. The screams and shouts led her there. She stepped into the room just as several doormen and bartenders, all carrying pistols, started toward the staircase.

Landrum and Glidinghawk—and Devlin—had to be upstairs.

Celia levered the Winchester and pointed it at the group of armed men. "Hold it!" she called.

They stopped and looked at her, clearly shocked to see a beautiful redhead covering them with a Winchester. Celia hoped they didn't notice how the barrel of the heavy rifle was shaking from the strain of holding it steady.

One of the bartenders said, "Lady, you'd better get out of here."

Celia shook her head. "Get away from the stairs."

The room was emptying rapidly as customers and inmates alike hurried out the front door, wanting to get as far away as possible before more trouble erupted. Celia was left facing the small group of Madam Henrietta's employees across a nearly deserted parlor.

More gunshots rang out from upstairs. Celia flinched as she heard the familiar crack of .44

Colts. Landrum's and Glidinghawk's?

"I said move!" she snapped.

She pressed the trigger of the rifle. It blasted hard against her shoulder, and the slug splintered a newel post on the banister of the staircase.

The men held on to their guns, but they moved away from the stairs. Celia had jacked another round into the chamber of the Winchester as soon as she fired the first shot, and she kept its muzzle trained on the men as she crossed the room and began to back up the stairs.

She didn't know what she was getting into, and her heart was pounding in fear, but she kept going.

As she reached the top of the stairs, a clanging sound came through the open front door. The local police were on their way, ringing the bells on their wagons, Celia thought.

That assumption seemed to be shared by the men still grouped near the bottom of the stairs, because they exchanged meaningful looks and then turned away, heading for the door just as the frightened customers had done. None of them wanted to be here when the police arrived.

Celia heard voices, heard the sound of footsteps hurrying down stairs. She turned as the door of Madam Henrietta's office opened.

Henrietta came out of the office, unsteady on her feet but clutching a small pistol tightly in her hand. She didn't see Celia because her attention was drawn by the sudden appearance of Devlin Henry, Landrum, Glidinghawk, and Fox as they came down the rear stairs from the third floor.

Henrietta raised the pistol toward them.

"Drop it!" Celia barked, settling the rifle's sight on Madam Henrietta's head.

The older woman looked over her shoulder and saw the Winchester lined up on her. A sick smile passed over her drawn face as she let the pistol slip from her hand.

Devlin spotted Celia and rushed down the hall toward her. Landrum covered Madam Henrietta while Glidinghawk scooped up the gun she had dropped.

Celia let the barrel of the rifle sag as Devlin took her in his arms. All the strain of the evening caught up with her then. The Winchester slipped completely out of her fingers as she let Devlin enfold her in his embrace.

The moment didn't last nearly long enough.

"We'd best get out of here," Landrum said. "This is all too complicated to be explaining to the local sheriff."

Devlin nodded reluctantly. "You're right." Looking at his former wife, who stood nearby with her head hanging in defeat, he said, "Judson and Roland are dead, Henrietta. I don't know how much you knew about their plans, but if I were you, I'd move on away from Denver as fast as I could."

Henrietta lifted her face long enough to say, "I don't intend to be here when the police arrive either."

Devlin nodded. His arm around Celia's shoulders tightened. "Let's go."

Celia glanced at Preston Fox and saw the bruises on his face. Other than that, he seemed to be all right, though. And none of the others appeared to be hurt. They had been very lucky, she knew.

As they reached the parlor, a door behind the bar suddenly opened. Landrum reacted instinctively, spinning that way and lifting his gun, but he held off as a young girl came reeling out of a narrow passageway. Her face was terribly battered, and she walked as if she was broken inside. She went to one knee as Celia gasped and hurried forward.

Celia caught the girl before she could fall. "My God," Celia said. "What happened to you?"

"The . . . the colonel . . ." the girl choked out. "When he . . . when he was through . . . with me . . . they shut me up . . . in a little room in the basement. . . . And then . . . when the shooting started . . . my guard ran out . . . I got the door open . . . Help me . . ."

Devlin knelt beside the girl as Celia held her. "Who did this to you? A colonel, you said?"

"I—I heard his name . . . Colonel Porter, they said . . ."

The bleak look on Devlin Henry's face at that moment was the most frightening thing she had ever seen, Celia thought.

There was a young trooper on guard duty in front of Colonel Matthias Porter's room at the Colorado House. He snapped to attention as Major Devlin Henry strode up, even though the major's uniform was disheveled and his face was grimed with powder smoke.

"I need to see the colonel, son," Devlin said quietly.

"I — I think the colonel has retired for the night, sir," the trooper replied. His voice was nervous as he went on, "Begging the major's pardon, sir, but I don't think the colonel would want to be disturbed. He seemed awful tired."

Considering what Porter had done to the girl named Ellen Franks, he should have been tired, Devlin thought grimly. But he said, "It's important, Private. I'll take the responsibility."

Without waiting any longer, Devlin stepped past the guard and pounded on the door.

A moment later, a groggy voice answered from within. "Who the devil's out there?"

Devlin glanced at the startled trooper and then grasped the doorknob and twisted it. He shoved the door open and stepped into the room.

Colonel Porter was lighting the lamp on the

bedside table as Devlin shut the door. With a disapproving frown, he snapped, "Major Henry, do you know what time it is? What the hell are you doing in my bedroom? Dammit, are you even going to salute?"

Devlin slipped the Colt from his holster and pointed it at the nightshirted colonel. "I don't salute a bastard like you," Devlin said in a voice that was deceptively soft.

Porter's eyes widened. "What the hell? Have you gone crazy, Henry? I'll have you court-martialed, you stupid son of a bitch!"

Devlin shook his head as he said, "I don't think so, Porter. You see, I've been talking to a girl named Ellen Franks."

"Who?" Porter demanded angrily.

"That's right. You probably wouldn't know her name. You didn't stop to ask it before you raped and beat her in Madam Henrietta's house earlier today."

Porter's face went pale in the harsh yellow light from the lamp. He stammered, "I—I don't know what you're t-talking about, mister—"

"I think you do." Devlin eared back the hammer of the Colt as Porter stirred in the bed. "Just stay still, or so help me I'll enjoy blowing your brains out. Ellen's in a private hospital now, and the doctor thinks she'll recover in plenty of time to testify against you. She heard quite a bit from that other room before Roland gave her to you.

She heard all about how you and Roland and Judson plotted to cheat the army and the country out of a fortune by leaking the commission's decision. Roland and Judson may have blackmailed you into joining their scheme because of your perversions, but that doesn't make you any less guilty than they were." Devlin's face tightened in a grimace as he thought about how he and the others had discovered Ellen Franks. "They were just out for profit. You're a monster, Porter!"

The colonel shook his head. "It's a lie, all of it, lies! You can't take the word of some . . . some little trollop!"

"It's good enough for me. And I think it'll be good enough for General Carruthers." Devlin paused and let that sink in. "He's the one who sent me out here to find the traitor on the commission."

The life went out of Porter's eyes as he realized the hopelessness of his position. At the very least, a court-martial and life imprisonment in the stockade were staring him in the face. At the worst — a firing squad . . .

Porter lunged for the holstered gun hanging on the chair beside the bed. Devlin cried, "Colonel! No!" as the man got his hand on the butt of the weapon.

Porter yanked the revolver free. Devlin hesitated, his finger taut on the trigger of his own Colt, giving the man every chance he could.

Colonel Matthias Porter jammed the muzzle of the pistol in his mouth and jerked the trigger.

Devlin stepped aside as the startled sentry burst into the room. The young trooper stopped in his tracks, gagging as he saw the bloody mess on the bed.

"I believe Colonel Porter has just relieved himself of command," Devlin said.

# CHAPTER TWENTY-ONE

She had met Devlin Henry on a train, Celia thought. It seemed fitting that she was saying good-bye to him as she was about to board another one.

"Don't worry about me," Devlin assured her. "General Carruthers himself is coming here to straighten everything out. With the testimony of that girl, all the questions should be cleared up. And you know I'm not in too much trouble, or the army wouldn't have placed me in temporary command of the commission."

"Where will you be going from here?" Celia asked, looking up at him. Steam was puffing up from the engine and the station's platform was crowded with passengers embarking and disembarking, but she tried to ignore all of that.

Devlin shook his head. "Who knows? Back to my regular duties, perhaps. I know one thing — I don't want anything more to do with these undercover assignments. I'm not cut out for that."

Celia's smile was bittersweet. Devlin might not feel comfortable with such missions, but for the moment, they were her life. She had thought long and hard on the matter, but in the end, she had made the decision that she couldn't leave Powell's Army . . . at least not yet.

Devlin still knew nothing of that part of her life. He had been convinced that everything she had done was simply to help him. He had accepted the story that she had run into Landrum and Glidinghawk and recruited them to help because she knew they had only recently joined the commission and couldn't be part of the plot against it.

At least he seemed to have accepted the story. If he did have any suspicions, Celia realized she would probably never know about them.

Fox had claimed to be a not-so-innocent bystander. His story was that he had been trying to rob the bank when Judson caught him there. Devlin had been tempted to turn him over to the sheriff, but that would have raised more questions than Devlin wanted to answer. He had settled for giving Fox a stern warning to get out of Denver, just as he had done with Madam Henrietta.

Henrietta was already gone, and no one knew where. Fox was on the train that was about to pull out, and he was not going to be eager to return to Denver anytime soon, not after the beating he had received at the hands of Judson and his henchman.

And the commission was scheduled to announce its decision for the site of the new fort within the week.

Somehow, through perseverance and sheer luck and with the help of Devlin Henry, Powell's Army had brought this mission to a successful conclusion.

But that didn't ease the hurt of parting, Celia thought.

She lifted her face to Devlin's as he took her in his arms. His kiss had all the passion and fire that she remembered so fondly. And perhaps one day she would taste it again. . . .

She lingered for a moment as the conductor yelled, "Boooard! All aboard!" Then she slipped out of his embrace and went to the steps of the car where her seat was located.

She went up the steps without looking back.

Celia knew if she looked back, she wouldn't be able to go.

The train was about a mile out of Denver when someone sat down in the empty seat beside Celia. She glanced over and saw Landrum Davis through the tears in her eyes.

Landrum didn't look at her. He kept his eyes straight ahead. But he said, "He was a good man. I'm glad we all turned out to be on the same side."

"Yes," Celia nodded. "I am, too." She tried to force herself to think of other things. "Where are

Gerald and Preston?"

Landrum chuckled. "Gerald's trying to talk Fox into letting him use some redskin remedy on his injuries. Claims it'll take care of those cuts and bruises right away."

"I'm sure Preston's not fond of that idea," Celia said with a smile. "Did you get any reply to that coded telegram you sent to Amos?"

"Not yet. I figured he'd want us to get out of Denver while everything's settling down, though. If I know Amos Powell, our next job will catch up to us soon enough."

"I hope so," Celia said. She lifted her chin and watched the spectacular Colorado scenery rolling by outside. She was ready for their next assignment. A little excitement would help her forget . . .

Or maybe not.